Treaty Brides

THE BRIGAND'S BRIDE

SAMANTHA CAYTO

The Brigand's Bride
ISBN # 978-1-80250-540-5

Interior text design by Claire Siemaszkiewicz
Pride Publishing

Published in 2023 by Pride Publishing, United Kingdom.

Pride Publishing is an imprint of Totally Entwined Group Limited.

Pride Publishing books by Samantha Cayto

Single Books

One Night in a Dungeon
Man Candy
Against a Rising Tide

Alien Slave Masters

The Captain's Pet
The Rebellious Pet
The Untamed Pet
The Captive Pet
The Inconvenient Pet
The Undercover Pet

Alien Blood Wars

Blood Dance
Dangerous Dance
Slave Dance
Star Dance
Mating Dance
Healing Dance
Smoke Dance
Final Dance: Part One
Final Dance: Part Two

Treaty Brides

Boi Bride
The Diplomat's Bride
Stolen Bride
The Substitute Bride
The Secret Bride
The Brigand's Bride

Anthologies

His Rules: Safeword
Right Here, Right Now: Never the Groom

Collections

Rules of Summer: In the Heat of the Dungeon
Dark and Deadly: Dream Demon
S.W.A.L.K.: His True Heart
His Harem: Room for Elijah

THE BRIGAND'S BRIDE

Chapter One

Evander had to choke back a whoop of excitement as he spied the carriage rumbling down the road. He and his men hadn't had such fruitful pickings in a long while, and though summer it might be, fall and winter would come soon enough. This ambush might yield considerable provisions for those in need to get through the hard seasons ahead. He swung down from the thick branches of his favorite perch and landed with a thud on the forest floor. Every bone in his body protested. *I'm getting too old for this.* It was no more than a passing thought. He couldn't stop, because the misery of those unable to protect themselves hadn't—and likely never would.

Nemo, his second in command, appeared out of thin air. They had a way of blending in with their surroundings. Despite their years together, Evander could still be startled by them…and that was good thing. If one wanted to lead a band of brigands, it helped to have someone for whom stealth was second nature. Nemo's short and thin stature was an asset, as well. It made it easier for them to hide behind trees and rocks, unlike Evander's tall, broad frame. Even a mountain would have trouble providing him cover. It hardly mattered. Here was where people in need depended on him, so this was where he'd stay. *And probably die.* But he never dwelled on such matters. His life meant nothing compared to the hundreds of others he served.

Nemo stood with their legs braced and arms crossed. "Someone is looking pleased with himself."

"Ha!" Evander clapped them on the shoulder. "Some rich person rides this way and without any outriders. I saw only one coachman and a footman on top."

"Soldiers could be hiding inside, ready to spring a counter ambush when we stop them." That was one of the better things about Nemo. They always assumed the worst.

"Unlikely, as the coach is too small. The most it could carry is four people. Hardly a challenge for us."

"I'll line up extra men, just in case."

"Fair enough."

As soon as Nemo disappeared back into the woods, Evander climbed the tree again to keep track of the coach's approach. Whoever was inside, and whatever the reason for them to travel this stretch of road that had gained a reputation of being populated by highwaymen, their pace indicated they were in no hurry. That was all to the good. It would allow Nemo to get everyone into position with time to spare. Evander was confident he'd arrive as usual to do the greeting, even if he stayed a bit longer to watch the carriage's progress. There was something about it... "Well, fuck me."

This was a chance he'd been hoping for since the last harsh winter. Simple robbery was no longer lucrative enough to satisfy the needs of those he helped. The dire situation required a bolder move, one that would produce far more coin in one fell swoop. It would be a tremendous escalation of their work, but one he wasn't completely comfortable with—nor had most of those who followed him been when he'd first broached the topic. Thieves, robbers, runaways and conmen they may be, but none of them had experience in what he now planned. The memory of all those starving faces from around the surrounding villages and farms helped him to harden his heart, however.

He scrambled down the tree and raced to the spot where they would deploy their ambush as shadowy figures—members of his band and loyal to him, one and all—arrived to take their positions. This time, he was going to ask much of them, and he wanted to have time to set them on the right path. It was going to be difficult, he knew. Nemo and the others turned to look at him with surprise as he hurried to join them. It wasn't in his nature to be rushed, but this situation wasn't normal. And he wanted to deliver the news as good fortune.

"The carriage belongs to the baron." He stood grinning with encouragement while his men absorbed the information and understood its importance.

Maurice was the first to get it. That was no surprise, given the man was high-born, even if it had been on the wrong side of the blanket. He had a sharp mind that was as good at tactics as Nemo was with logistics. "Our first chance for abduction has arrived, then. I wonder who's inside." The man had a face not unlike the proverbial hedge fence, but when he smiled, his blue eyes crinkled in an appealing way.

Evander shrugged. "Who, indeed? Someone worthy of a carriage instead of a wagon or a saddle-sore ride through the woods."

The information finally clicked for Nemo. "It could be no one of great importance. Maybe the tax collector has broken his leg and needs a carriage to get around for his dirty work. For his own purposes, the baron would certainly want his man to do his duty quickly."

"Possibly," Evander allowed. He didn't think so, however. That particular man was smart enough to know this road was a danger to him. They'd robbed him often in the early years. There were others that, while inconvenient, provided a safer route, and the tax collector had taken to using those. "We can only know by doing what we do best, and once we do, I'll make a decision of how to proceed."

"You mean to take the occupant hostage and ransom them?" This from Brother Manfred. The man was dressed for battle as usual, with his short sword tucked into his belt looped around his robe that served as a tunic. But his role was only ever to soothe frayed nerves as their victims were liberated of their wealth. His kindly face, lined with age and accented with a meticulous goatee, helped travelers believe it when they were told they wouldn't be harmed. His obvious tie to the nearby monastery helped, as well, although if they only knew what went on in that dark place, they wouldn't feel so calm around him. Fortunately for all of them, Manfred had fled the naked cruelty and avarice of the monastery. He was the most decent man Evander had ever known and the keeper of his band's collective conscience. That was the problem now, regrettably.

"I do," Evander confirmed. "The person in that carriage may be our first and only chance at extorting a sufficiently large amount of money to see our people through the coming winter. It's a happy circumstance if the funds come from the baron, himself and not one of the fawning nobles he rules over."

Manfred shook his head. "I've been against this scheme since you first contemplated it, as you know. Robbery is one thing, but kidnapping crosses the line. How do we look ourselves in our own reflections, never mind explaining it to those whom we help?"

Nemo spoke up. "When it means their children are not starving, they won't care. It's not like we're going to kill anyone."

Manfred frowned. "What if the occupant is a woman? How will she fare, living rough in the forest with us for the many days it will take for a ransom to arrive?"

Evander tried not to sigh. They'd had this discussion, or variations of it, before. Every issue Manfred raised was a valid one. They simply paled in comparison to the suffering of so many others. "Mabel and Cath manage, as well as the rest of us." He gestured toward the women, who stood ready with their bows. "And Susannah will know how to make a female guest comfortable." The keeper of their camp was a strong woman for all her tender years and soft demeanor.

"You'll get no argument from me about the strength and skill of our female comrades, Evan. They are not, however, noblewomen, as any woman in that carriage is likely to be. She will be used to finery and pampering and not, frankly…shitting in the woods."

"She'll get used to it," Mabel interjected. "It's not that hard—not as much as being beaten and raped." Like many of his 'men', Mabel had fled from an untenable life, where living rough in the forest and robbing passersby was a glorious life in comparison.

Putting his hands on his hips, Manfred shot her a sympathetic look. "I should hope we can do far better than that in our treatment of others." He turned his attention back to Evander. "I have a bad feeling about this."

Evander put a hand on the man's shoulder. "I understand your concern, and I can't say I am entirely happy about the idea myself. I don't want any of you to do that which your conscience cannot abide. Let us make a compromise and agree that if the occupant of the carriage is a woman, we take her money and nothing else. If it's a man"—he closed his eyes a moment—"we have to do more to help our people."

Maurice clapped his hands and rubbed them together. "A fine plan, Evan." He glanced around at the others. "Well, what are you waiting for? Get into position, everyone." There was only a moment's hesitation before the rest did as Maurice said.

Evander squeezed Manfred's shoulder. "Are we good, Brother?"

The man nodded once. "Aye, I suppose so, but I still think this is a mistake. Bringing a stranger to our camp will be dangerous, and he'll require constant guarding."

"Agreed." Evander let go. "And as this is my idea and my responsibility, I will look after our guest in all ways. If it fails, it will be my fault and no one else's."

"I can only pray to the gods we will succeed."

Relieved that there was no more disagreement on the matter, Evander said, "I thought you no longer believed in the gods." *And who would, after what you witnessed in the monastery?*

"I don't, but it doesn't hurt to ask for help, just in case."

With a laugh, Evander headed to his usual place in an ambush, pushing away the doubt he felt in his heart.

* * * *

Rory stared out at the endless monotony of the forest. He'd never been so far from home, yet he found nothing exciting about his trip. It was boring and uncomfortable. His father had only spared the oldest carriage he had, with weak springs and lumpy seats. And what he expected to find at the end of the journey didn't give him any hope of something better. He expected University City to be more frightening than anything else. Still, tedium was the immediate problem. "Will we never get there?" He didn't bother to hide his peevishness. He was still within his father's reach, and everyone expected such an attitude of him, anyway.

His valet, Maxwell, gave him the sort of stern look that he employed with impunity. "We've been gone less than two days, sir. It takes at least five to get to our destination."

Rory rolled his eyes. The old man was tiresomely right—always—and never shied away from delivering hard truths. There was some comfort in the routine, and it would be much harder to make the journey without him—not that Rory would ever admit such a thing. As far as he was concerned, Maxwell was just as guilty about the misery that his life had become as his parents were. It might not be fair to blame a servant, but the man was the safest place to concentrate his anger. "You might have devised a way to amuse me while we plod along."

"Would you like me to sing some bawdy tavern songs? I know quite a few." The old man's face remained as placid as ever.

Rory dismissed his ridiculous question with the scoff it deserved and went back to staring out of the window. This forest sitting on the outskirts of his father's holding was vast, dark and foreboding. No human with an ounce of sanity would make their home here, given that it was populated with all manner of large and dangerous creatures—or so he'd heard. Still, it held a certain fascination. A person could leave the known world behind and lose themselves within its thickness. *What would happen if I jumped out of the carriage right now and ran into these woods?* Would his father's men even bother to stop and chase after him? *Probably not. Good riddance to him. That's what they would think.* Well, perhaps Maxwell might do so, out of loyalty to Rory's dead mother, if nothing else.

Shaking his head, Rory dismissed the impulse. It never helped to imagine a life other than the one he was leading. "Do you think there are monsters living in the forest?" It was a silly question, but he was bored.

Maxwell drew in a breath, a clear sign that his patience was being tested. "There are no monsters, sir."

Rory was considering a retort about how wrong that was, as he'd lived with a few his entire life, when the carriage lurched to a halt. Shouts penetrated the glass window of the door. He grabbed the edge of his seat. "What's that? What's happening?"

Grim-faced, Maxwell peered outside. "Brigands, sir."

"We're being robbed." It wasn't a question, but others bounced around his mind, mostly concerning whether this outcome had been the plan all along when he'd been sent on the journey.

The door opened abruptly, revealing a sharp arrow notched and pointing generally in his direction. "Everybody out, if you please." The voice issuing the order was surprisingly cultured, not the rough speech of a workman. A large hand with long fingers that didn't belong to the archer beckoned them. "Now, if you please. Otherwise, I'll have to come in and drag you out." The tone of the man implied that he would find such a move bothersome.

Before Rory could make himself move, Maxwell leaned forward and climbed out of the carriage. "If it's money you're after—and I can only assume it is—I have access to it." The man uttered a muffled grunt of outrage and disappeared from Rory's line of sight.

That hand reappeared and beckoned again. "Your servant is not enough. Come now. My patience is wearing thin."

Rory had long ago mastered the art of hiding his fears and using contempt to deal with bullies. He forced himself to step out of the carriage with his head held high. His fast-beating heart made it hard to maintain his expression of disdain, but he could do it. A façade of indifference was his only defense. His well-honed control stuttered to a halt when he saw his attacker for the first time. A man much older than he, yet still significantly younger than Maxwell, stood with his hand on the hilt of a sheathed knife. Tall and broad, the brigand was an impressive man, even though he wore a tunic and trousers that had seen better days. Dark brown hair hung in shaggy layers nearly down to his shoulders. His unkempt look showed no signs of him having lived a life of luxury. Although his clean-shaven face didn't have the florid and soft look of Rory's father, his weathered skin was nevertheless smooth-looking, and his brown eyes were clear. When he smiled at Rory, he showed straight, white teeth. This was no ordinary highwayman.

"Thank you for joining us, my lord. It's such a lovely day, much better to talk outside than in that stuffy carriage."

"I'm not a lord." Rory bit out the truth from habit. Folding his arms, he tried to give the man a look of disdain. It was hard to do so. There was something compelling about the brigand that disturbed and cowed him. Rory didn't want to stare into his eyes.

"I beg your pardon." The man gave him a baiting smile, then tapped the outside of the door. "This is the baron's crest, is it not?" When Rory said nothing, he continued with a narrow-eyed gaze. "The baron has three sons, I believe."

Rory tugged at his frizzy braid, not sure how to respond. But anyone who had ever seen the baron knew that Rory's curly, red hair was not usual. His pale skin, dotted as it was with freckles along the bridge of his nose, made him an outlier among his family, as well. "Do I look like a son of the baron?"

"Yes, actually." The brigand startled him by flicking a finger at Rory's sleeve. "Such fine dress speaks of nobility." He used that same finger to catch Rory's necklace and give it a gentle tug. "And this jewelry is worth a pretty price."

Rory wrenched away. "Don't touch that!" His abrupt movement would have sent him tumbling to his ass on the carriage step if the brigand hadn't caught him by the elbow. Rory pulled free. "And don't touch me!"

"My apologies, sir. I didn't mean to alarm you. We don't steal that which has obvious sentimental value. We seek money, first and foremost."

Rory clasped his palm against the necklace. *How does he know what it means to me?* "My valet has already told you he keeps the coin. It's in the strongbox up with the coachman. Take what you want and let us go on our way."

"Why, thank you very much, kind sir." The man's tone mocked, but his eyes twinkled as if Rory were in on the joke and not the butt of it. "We've already liberated that. There is something else, however, that will fill our coffers even more."

"Wh-what are you talking about?" He didn't like the look in the man's eye.

"You."

"Me?" Rory's voice squeaked, which was embarrassing but he was too shocked to care. "You can't be serious."

"Oh, but I am. You are the baron's son, of that I'm sure. He'll pay a pretty price to get you back, I'll wager."

Rory nearly laughed at the absurd notion. The baron wouldn't pay anything. The old goat probably wouldn't piss on him if he were on fire. Saying as much, however, wasn't going to help. No one, other than Maxwell, would believe him. He was going to be taken hostage, no matter what he said. *Then I'll die in this horrid forest for certain.* Fearful and unable to explain the futility of his abduction, he lashed out as he'd learned to do when frightened and cornered. "You can't have me, you brute!" He kicked at the man's crotch and clawed at his face, even knowing it could lead to his quick death.

Instead of stopping him with the point of his knife, the brigand merely avoided his assault, captured his arms in a strong grip, spun him around and wrestled him into a tight hug. The despicable robber had the temerity to laugh as he did so. Rory thrashed and pounded at the man's arms, but to no avail. It didn't take long for him to become exhausted at the effort, and in the end, he lay limp and panting in his grasp.

"If you are done trying to escape the inevitable, we shall take our leave now." The words were said not unkindly.

Resigned temporarily to his fate, Rory didn't struggle as the brigand hauled him away from the carriage. Another man, surprisingly dressed as a monk, approached. "Evan, let me tend to the boy. He's little more than a child."

"I am *not* a child." He'd always had trouble guarding his tongue, but this was a sore topic for him. He knew his short stature and lack of facial hair made him look young and helpless. Those assumptions by others made him vulnerable. To prove his point, he started to struggle again.

The man called 'Evan' tightened his grip. "Thank you but no. This is my burden to bear—and it's not as bad as it looks." The man's laughing tone was clear.

Rory tried to kick backward, pressing himself against the man's body. That's when he felt a frightening hardness. A shiver streaked down his spine, and he went limp again. This was a danger he hadn't contemplated. Now that it was obvious, he didn't want to do anything to encourage the man's interest.

"Wise boy." The words were nearly a whisper against his ear.

The sound of them, coupled with the tickling warm breath against his skin, made Rory shiver again. His breathing came in quick pants that he labored to get under control. *Show no fear.* That was a lesson hard learned, and it would serve him well in this situation.

"You, valet, take my words back to the baron. He's to have a half-year's-worth of taxes to be delivered to this spot in a fortnight if he wishes to see his son again."

Maxwell drew himself up straight and looked down at the brigand as only the man could, despite his shorter stature. "I will do no such thing. The coachman will take back the message. I go where my young master does."

That caused the ruffians around them to laugh. "The boy won't have need of your pampering service," the leader said. "We live rough in the forest. The experience might do him some good, actually."

Rory didn't know what to say or what to do. He'd never been without Maxwell, and as hard as he could be on the devoted servant, the thought of being without his company was terrifying. Only pride kept him from sending the man a pleading look or speaking up to keep him.

It didn't matter, in any event. Maxwell wasn't to be deterred. "Take me with you, or I shall find a way to follow." His gaze slanted sideways toward the archers still pointing arrows at them. "Regardless of the potential consequences."

"Will the baron pay more for us to release you, as well?"

"No." Maxwell's expression and tone never changed from his determined haughtiness. The man had courage. There was no denying that.

Rory knew a measure of gratitude and tried to show it in his eyes before saying, "He means it. The stubborn old man has always been a thorn in my side, but he does have his uses."

There was silence while everyone waited for the leader of the brigands to decide. His chest rose and fell against Rory's back on a big sigh. "Very well. It might make my job easier, I suppose." He stepped away from the carriage, dragging Rory with him. "Turn around and go back to the baron with my demands," he shouted to the coachman and footman.

They were two of the laziest servants in the baron's household, but they would high-tail it back to the safety of the castle, that was for certain. Their message would fall on deaf ears, however. Rory knew that for sure and so did Maxwell, no doubt. Perhaps the man wanted to join the brigands rather than continue to serve the baron or Rory. No one could blame him if that were the case.

They waited until the carriage was back on its way before the brigands lowered their weapons and celebrated their success with muted grins and back-slapping. A large, homely man tossed the coin purse in his large hand. "A decent haul, Evan, even without the ransom."

"Good. We shall wait for the baron to send us more. Come, young sir. I will show you to your temporary home." He loosened his grip enough for Rory to walk by his side, although he still held him close.

As he stepped off the road and into the dark shadows of the forest, Rory hid his fear with bravado. "You will rue this decision to kidnap me."

The brigand squeezed Rory's waist. "Oh, I doubt it. I'm already enjoying my time with you."

Rory managed to jab his elbow into the oaf's stomach. "You will keep your hands to yourself."

The brigand merely chuckled, even as he rubbed the spot where the elbow had landed. "I do love a challenge, but worry not, young sir. No one will harm you here. You have my word on it."

"As if that means anything."

The man didn't respond right away. "It has to. I have little else left to give." And on that odd declaration, they continued making their way deeper into the woods in silence.

Chapter Two

Evander kept his grip on his hostage as they made their way to the band's current camp. He didn't trust that the boy wouldn't run at the first opportunity, and more than worrying about losing out on the ransom, he believed that the bratty nobleman would get himself hopelessly lost. There was no thicker, bigger or more dangerous forest in all Moorcondia. Unless one knew the area well, it all looked similar, and the sources of fresh water were few and well-hidden. Only the Dark Mountains were a worse place to navigate, in his opinion. Years of making their home in the woods had given him and his followers a good internal map of the area. Even they, however, were careful not to venture too far beyond the familiar perimeter without careful planning. This slip of a boy would never find his way back to the road unless he were incredibly lucky. So, Evander held on to only as much of Rory's arm as was necessary, although truth be told, he had rather enjoyed holding him flush against his body.

Too much so.

He was still hard from the experience, and this meager touch did nothing to dispel it. Thank the gods his tunic hid his arousal, but Rory had felt it. The way the boy's heart had thumped and his breath quickened, Evander could imagine it was caused by desire and not fear. That was a foolish wish on his part. The baron's son had made it very clear that he considered all of them scum. Even if Evander was interested in a dalliance and the boy seemed to acquiesce, the situation made it impossible. He could never be sure whether the boy truly wanted him or gave in because he wanted to curry favor with his captor. Evander would do well to remember the imbalance of power between them. Damn, it had been a long time since he'd bedded anyone, and Rory was an unexpected temptation.

The boy stumbled, then righted himself without Evander's help. "Damn it, how far are we going? My boots are being ruined." His tone implied it was the worst possible event.

Evander spared them a glance. "Nothing a good brush and polish won't fix."

"Shows what you know. These aren't farmer's boots. They are made from the finest leather."

"I'm sure your father will buy you a new pair when he has you back. Just as I'm sure you'll make your manservant tend to them during your stay." He didn't add 'poor bastard'. The older man walked stoically behind them, his severe, black clothing implying he was a no-nonsense type of person. Evander doubted there would ever be complaints coming from him. If anything, he might decide to remain with them. His lot of catering to the baron's spoiled child couldn't be a happy one. And yet, there had been a fierceness in his eyes when he'd demanded to be brought along. There was something about his relationship with the boy that went beyond merely a servant doing his duty.

Rory tugged at Evander's hold. "It would be easier for me to avoid the mud if you let go. I don't need to be guided like a child."

"We'll have to disagree on that point."

The boy scowled. "How much longer?"

Evander held back a sigh. *And to think we worried about kidnapping a woman.* "Not so very long—in time for supper, in fact."

"I'm sure it will be delectable."

The snide comment bothered him more than he let on. Susannah toiled all day, every day, to feed his band. It was her skill and one she enjoyed doing—especially as no one gave her the back of their hand if they didn't like what she'd prepared or she was late in getting it done. If nothing else, he prided himself on how every member of his band was valued, and no one lived in fear of him or anyone else.

This deep in the forest, the canopy didn't let in much sun, giving their surroundings an eerie patina. A fox let out a screech, making his captive startle and bump into him. For a few delightful seconds, he stayed plastered to Evander's side. Not only did Evander's dick respond as it had before, but his protective instincts also kicked in. This boy might be a spoiled brat, but that didn't make his fear any less legitimate. He really hated to give him a reason to move away again, but he was a fair-minded man, not a user and abuser unlike many of the nobility.

"It's only a fox. I know it sounds like a woman screaming, does it not? Have you never heard one before?"

Rory did move away and feigned—to Evander's way of looking at it—indifference. "I suppose I have. I guess I didn't realize who—what—was making it."

An odd answer. It was hard to read the boy's expression from the side, but even with that vantage point, Evander thought he saw sadness. Although Rory wasn't part of the band, he was Evander's responsibility, nevertheless. He had a duty to reassure him. "I won't let anyone or anything hurt you while you're with me."

Rory flicked his gaze at him. "Does that include you?"

Evander stopped abruptly enough to cause the boy to stumble. He righted him again and shifted him so that he could stare into his eyes. "Of course, it does. I know you have no reason to believe me, but all I want is the ransom. I will not take advantage of you in any way."

The boy seemed to consider his words, his gaze dropping and a curious look on his face. "I suppose I have no choice but to accept your reassurance." He lifted his chin and stared back at him. "I'm powerless. That doesn't mean I'm complacent, however."

Evander lifted his eyebrows. "I never expected you were."

While the rest of his men had gone on ahead of them, the servant had stopped. He waited with the look of a man ready to remain in that position until the end of time. His patience was remarkable, although once again, Evander sensed that something more than duty was keeping him by his young master's side.

When they had reached the camp, Evander lead his captive over to the spot where he kept his belongings and laid his head down at night. Judging that the boy was boxed in enough with everyone gathered, he let go in order to unfurl his pallet. "This is where you will stay while you are our…during your stay with us." It really wouldn't be fair of him to refer to the boy as a 'guest' when he was there by force. No one would appreciate such an obvious lie, and there was no reason to be unduly provocative.

Rory stood with his arms crossed, staring at Evander's meager possessions and privacy. "You can't expect me to sleep here." His expression had turned more mulish than it had been during the walk.

"I do, yes."

The boy looked around. "You mean to say that all of you live rough like this? Have you no…hut, tent, cave or anything remotely civilized to live in?"

Evander ignored the eye-rolling and snickers from his people. This kidnapping venture had been his idea, and even those who had gotten behind it no doubt considered any related problem his to deal with. "We need to be nimble. Your father has sent soldiers into these woods many times to find us. Everything we have can be packed quickly, carried easily and left behind if necessary. So no, we have nothing but what you see."

"What do you do when it rains?" The privileged boy actually stamped his foot.

At the end of his patience, Evander leaned toward him. "We get wet and sometimes cold. Now sit and be quiet."

Oh, the lad didn't like that at all. After a few fuming seconds, he stomped over to the pallet and plopped his pert ass down. Interestingly, he seemed careful to keep his muddy boots off the cloth. His gaze roamed the camp site, taking everything in with a keener eye than Evander would have expected.

I must not let my guard down with this one.

The old servant walked over to his young master. "Let me take those boots off you, sir, and see what I can do to make them more presentable." At a curt nod, he kneeled beside the pallet and wrested the boots from Rory's small and narrow feet and went to lean against a nearby tree to take stock of what the damage was.

Evander got the sudden and hopefully absurd thought that the man might lick the leather clean. He'd known cruel masters who demanded exactly that. To be sure that didn't happen, he pulled out a rag that he used for his sword and dagger whenever they got dirty and handed it to the servant. "You may use this."

"Thank you, sir. And my name is Maxwell." He gave a shallow bow.

"I am Evander, Evan to my friends. Feel free to use it—both of you," he added with a flick of his gaze toward Rory. "I may be the leader here, but we subscribe to a more egalitarian way of life."

Rory snorted. "So you *are* the chief kidnapper. Very nice for you, I'm sure, *Evan*."

The snotty tone grated on Evander's last nerve. It was a struggle to remember that the boy had every right to be furious with him. Small denigrations of him paled in comparison to the effrontery of snatching someone and holding them against their will. When he took a step forward to say…something, the valet stopped him with a hand on his arm.

"Please do not take offense at my master's words. He's had a difficult day, as I'm sure you can imagine. If there is punishment to be meted out for his sharp tongue, please consider me to be at fault. I am responsible for my charge's actions." He held his head high as if to demonstrate his courage.

The people around them went suddenly quiet, and Evander couldn't quite keep his jaw from dropping. "Don't tell me that in addition to his other vicious acts, the baron employs the concept of a whipping boy."

The man said nothing. But Rory surprised Evander by jumping to his feet. "Don't you dare touch him! I can take my licks myself but be warned that I will not let you lay your filthy hands on me without a fight."

Evander slowly looked from Rory to Maxwell and back again. Nobleman and servant had a strange dynamic. One thing for sure was that the boy wasn't entirely self-centered and petulant—or perhaps he simply didn't like the idea of Evander touching his property. No matter. The day had been long, and the night promised to be longer still.

He waved his hand. "Just stay where you are."

He walked over to Maurice and Nemo, who stood watching the drama play out with obvious glee. "Do *not* say it," he snapped.

Manfred came to join them. "They won't but I will. This is a disaster in the making, Evander." He kept his voice low so that their discussion wouldn't reach prying ears. "I blame myself. I should have anticipated that someone vulnerable other than a woman should be left alone. It bears repeating that this son of the baron is practically still a child."

Evander eyed his captive. "He's young, I'll grant you, but he's full grown. Or at least, he's an adult. It's hard to believe he'll stay that small and delicate. Quite fetching, really." His train of thought popped out before he could stop it.

Maurice snorted. "And he's going to be cuddled up next you for some nights to come, heh, Evan?"

"You will leave him be," Nemo shot out before Manfred did.

"Of course I will." Evander didn't bother to hide his irritation. "I hope you know me better than that." When Nemo merely stared back at him. "I will not lay a hand on that boy, but I must keep him close. If he takes off, he'll be in great danger. You know this."

* * * *

Rory stared down at the bowl of soup Maxwell handed him and wrinkled his nose. "Is this cabbage?"

"Yes, sir. Also potatoes, carrots, leeks and some dried venison."

"It smells revolting." He knew he was being unfair, but he'd also learned that if he didn't speak up for himself, he was always going to be handed the short end of the stick. *Not that complaining gets me anywhere, either.*

"I assure you, sir, it is quite tasty. I took the liberty of testing it myself, and it is what everyone else is eating. You are not being singled out for special treatment." To anyone hearing those words, they might think the man meant that Rory wasn't going to get anything better than anyone else. He and Maxwell knew, however, that it was the opposite. These brigands weren't treating him like a hound sitting under the table waiting for scraps.

He sniffed the soup again before dipping his spoon into the murky liquid and bringing some of it to his lips. One tentative sip told him that it did taste good. And gods, he was starving. It took well-honed restraint for him to eat it slowly, as if he were doing his captors a favor by eating it. His small stomach filled quickly, so one bowl left him feeling satisfied.

He held the empty bowl out to Maxwell. "It was palatable. Did you get enough?" he asked belatedly. His servant was an unexpected addition to the brigands' scheme. Nothing said they had to bother feeding him.

"Yes, sir. The keeper of the camp, Susannah, was most obliging." The old man looked around them. "These people have showed me a measure of kindness, truth be told."

Rory snorted. "Of course they have. You're a downtrodden servant. I bet they've already tried to recruit you to their cause." He tried not to show how much he cared about that. This miserable situation wasn't going to end well for him. He had to accept that truth, but there was hope that Maxwell would emerge unscathed and with others to depend on. For sure, he would never return to the baron.

"They have not, nor would I entertain such an offer."

Rory stared the man in the eyes. "You should. I don't have to tell you what the future holds. If there's a chance for you to join them, I advise you to take it."

Maxwell peered down at him with a frankness that he rarely showed. "You think I would throw my lot in with these brigands if they harm you?" He straightened. "I made a vow to your mother, and that alone dictates my course of action."

Rory didn't bother to point out that no one knew what he'd promised and no one would likely care, in any event. If the old man wasn't going to take his advice, there was nothing to be done about it. Perhaps when the time came, he would decide differently. The point of a sword had a way of changing even the most stubborn of minds.

"Do as you like. I don't care." Rory looked away and wrapped his arms around his knees.

"I shall see to the cleaning of your bowl and spoon and return to prepare you for your slumber."

Rory said nothing, keeping his gaze in constant motion to take in as much of his prison as he could. He didn't have long—a fortnight, perhaps a few days more than that. If there were a chance at escape, he would have to at least try. The forest was a frightening place, but at least it held some hope. None of that would be forthcoming here. His gaze landed on the leader. The man sat among some of his band, done eating apparently, and no doubt discussing the luck of their day. They'd probably expected no more than a wealthy merchant to grab. Having the son of the baron must seem to them as if their dreams had come true. *If they only knew.*

The leader's gaze slid from one of his companions to land on Rory. For a moment, they stared at each other. There was nothing all that special about the man. His hair was an unremarkable brown and looked in need of a good trimming. His eyes were some shade of brown, as well. Handsome enough but not like the pretty and fawning hangers-on at the baron's castle. No women were going to swoon at the sight of him, but they probably wouldn't say no to a tumble if he asked. There was really no reason for a shiver to go down Rory's spine...yet it did. Uncomfortable, he looked away and stared at the ground until Maxwell returned.

There was little to do in the way of preparing him for bed. He had no change of clothing and didn't want to make the journey to whatever served as the privy in this awful place. No doubt, he'd be escorted by that damnable man—and that wouldn't do. The humiliation would have to be faced in the morning, of course. He simply didn't have the energy to do so at the moment. When he lay down on the pallet, his back noticed the rough hardness of the ground that the thin pad couldn't disguise. There was no pillow other than his arm, and as he rolled to his side to find a comfortable position, he resigned himself to a terrible night—the first of many to come.

Maxwell positioned himself at Rory's feet, the pallet long enough to accommodate the man, given how short Rory was. His valet hadn't put his head down for more than a few seconds when the brigand leader strode over.

"Get up, old man. This isn't where you're sleeping."

Maxwell sat up. "I always sleep by my master."

"Not here, you don't." The man gestured with his thumb toward the big brute who'd followed him. "You'll stay with Maurice, as I have no wish to have to safeguard you both. Don't worry," he added when Maxwell hesitated. "I'm sure the boy can wipe his own ass for a few days."

Rory gasped in outrage and sat bolt upright. "You are disgusting. And if you think I'm going to spend the night lying beside your big, oafish body..." Rory snapped his mouth shut and swallowed a grunt when his captor simply lay down beside him. The pallet had seemed so wide up until that moment. Now it was far too narrow, the man nearly touching him from shoulder to foot.

Rory tried to ignore the massive body lying too close to him. He even inched his way to the far edge of the pallet, but any farther and he'd land on the ground entirely. He was contemplating that very move when his captor flicked a quilt over the both of them. The fabric was worn, testament to its age and hard use, no doubt, so there wasn't that much warmth to be had from it. Still, it did help, and more, it forced his body to remain next to the brigand's. Any effort now to escape the uncomfortable closeness would result in losing the covering. With the chill of the night air already seeping under his skin, he was loathe to lose what little comfort he had.

It doesn't matter anyway. If he's intent on violating me, no amount of distance between us will stop him.

He lay stiffly on his back, peering up at the dark canopy of the forest and listening to the low murmurs of the others in the camp as they too retired. In his own chambers back in the baron's castle, he fell asleep to the raucous sounds of powerful men reveling long after the evening meal had ended. The noise never disturbed him because it was all he'd ever known. Here in these woods, it was surprisingly quiet in comparison, except for the occasional hooting of an owl and what he now knew was the cry of a fox. It should have been easier to fall asleep in such a relatively muffled environment, yet somehow it wasn't. Perhaps it was the brigand's presence and the effect that it had on his nerves. The proximity of the man's body was like an itch along his skin, even though they weren't quite touching. The sensation was something he wanted to scratch at yet couldn't. Any movement would cause him to brush up again the man, and the last thing he wanted was for his abductor to think he wanted him.

"You think too loudly."

The sound of the brigand's voice startled him. "What a ridiculous thing to say." He braced himself for what might come next, as obviously the man was wide awake and concentrating his attention on him.

"You need to relax and go to sleep. I'm sure you're tired from your...difficult day. And as I've already assured you, you need not have any fear of me. I won't touch you in the way that you would worry about. I'm not a despoiler of innocence. You're safe here, so long as you make no attempt to escape."

Rory couldn't hold back a snort. "You and I have very different ideas of what it means to be safe. And yes, you could say that my day has been *difficult*. 'Horrific' would be a more accurate description, however."

The brigand sighed and shifted a hairbreadth away from him. "My apologies. You are right, of course. This is bad business, and I can only say in my defense that I do this to help ensure that as few people starve this coming winter as possible. You probably don't realize how harsh your father is with those living on his land. He bleeds them dry," he added with an edge of anger seeping into his tone.

"I know what the baron is like." Rory had hardened his heart to the suffering of others for purposes of self-preservation. Hearing it laid out in such stark terms made it impossible to dismiss, but his stomach tightened with the sure knowledge that this venture of the brigand wasn't going to help matters.

"Then perhaps you can at least understand why I took you, even if it would be too much to ask for you to accept your circumstances with good grace."

Rory grimaced into the darkness. "Yes, it is too much to ask. I hate this, and I hate you." As he said the words, he wasn't sure that was entirely true. It was hard to fault those who fought against the baron's evilness. Still, he couldn't ignore the fact that he was lying next to the man who in all likelihood was going to end his life. *Or he'll order someone else to do it.* No. Unlike the baron, the brigand was the kind of man who took care of his problems himself. Although he hardly knew him, Rory was sure of his assessment.

"You're entitled to your feelings. Just don't try to escape during the night. I'm a light sleeper and will know if you get up. And if somehow I don't, you are going to get lost out there on your own. You might think now that it's a better alternative than staying with me, but there are plenty of beasts roaming around at night, looking for their next meal. Small as you are, you'd make a tasty snack for a bear or a pack of wolves."

At that very moment, a distant roar made Rory jerk toward the brigand, as if he were a safe haven and not a horrible kidnapper. "What was that?"

The man had the temerity to chuckle. "One of those bears I just spoke about, one with perfect timing. I was not exaggerating. Now, go to sleep, little lord."

"I'm *not* a lord." The man surely understood title conventions when it came to nobility and was only trying to dig at him. It was irksome, but he was tired and nothing would be gained from staying awake. Closing his eyes, he willed himself to relax. Worrying never made anything better. No one knew that better than he. And soon all his problems would be over—along with his life.

Chapter Three

Evander woke with the dawn, as was his habit, although he wasn't used to having a raging hard-on as he did so. This morning was different. His dick pressed painfully against the fly of his trousers, demanding to be tended to in a way that it rarely did. When he'd started his band of brigands, he'd promised himself that he wasn't going to let his personal needs intrude on his leadership. The idea was to form a better society, one where the powerful didn't exploit and prey on those less fortunate. Even if he believed any of his people were interested in him, he could never be sure if they came to his pallet out of true desire or to placate him as they'd learned to do with other men. It wasn't something he was willing to risk, and with their existence almost entirely being apart from others, his hand was the only source of pleasure his cock had found in these last few years.

The rest of the camp began to stir as none of them had come from a life where they had the luxury of lying abed. Everyone rose from their respective pallets and got on with the chores of everyday living, except for the boy lying next to him. The baron's son had oddly turned toward him, not away. He lay on his side, his arm acting as a pillow, something he was undoubtedly used to having. His brow was furrowed, even in sleep, probably due to a bad dream. *Caused by me, most likely.* Evan wanted to rub his thumb along the lines to smooth them out. He stopped himself just as his hand lifted of its own volition, testament to how his feelings were getting ahead of his brain.

When the boy's lips started moving in obvious agitation, Evander pushed himself up on one arm. "Wake up, little lord." He made his voice stern yet kept it low.

Rory woke in the next instant, his gaze roving around. "What?" He blinked a few times before looking at Evan. "Oh." That was all he said before sitting up and rubbing the sleep from his eyes with what appeared to be a shaky hand.

"Sorry to disturb your beauty sleep, but we rise early." That was certainly true, except that was not the reason he'd roused the boy. He was sure the lad wouldn't appreciate being told he was woken to break the throes of his unpleasant dream. Evan stood, irritated with his erection. The damn thing wasn't deflating. "Come on. I'll take you to the privy."

Rory didn't move right away, and as he got to his feet, he seemed unsteady. When he stumbled, Evan reached out to keep him from falling. The moment his hands touched the desirable boy, his dick jerked with enthusiasm.

Fortunately, it was Rory who broke the contact right away. "I don't need your help." He stepped away from the pallet with his back straight and no more wobbling. "Where is this privy?"

Evan gestured. "We've dug a trench over this way. Come. I'll take you."

"As you've already so crudely put it, I don't need anyone to wipe my ass, thank you very much." A look of red-faced fury crossed the boy's face. His cheeks remained rosy from it.

Evan strived for patience. "I understand how difficult this is for you, but until your father pays the ransom, it is my responsibility to ensure that you remain safe and sound. I promise I have no designs on your backside for any reason." That wasn't entirely true. As he said the words, an image of sinking his cock into that small and undoubtedly tight backside popped into his head. He had to bite back a groan. Grabbing the boy's upper arm, he led him from the camp, ignoring the lad's struggles to break free of his grip.

The trench that they'd dug was far enough away for the stench not to bother them in the camp. As they approached it, Sammy, a boy not yet in the full bloom of manhood, passed them. "I put fresh rushes down, sir." He beamed at him. Before joining them, the poor thing had known little more than the back of someone's hand or the sting of a belt.

"Good lad." Evan ruffled Sammy's hair, pleased that he no longer flinched when he saw the hand coming. "Tell Susannah I said you've earned your breakfast." Understanding the jest, the boy laughed and ran back to the camp.

Rory, on the other hand, managed to jerk his arm to free it. "What am I going to have to do to earn mine?" He sneered at Evan, but there was fear more than anger in his eyes.

"Nothing. My comment to the boy was meant as no more than a humorous sally. He knew as much." He sighed as he moved them along to the privy. "I know you have no reason to believe me, but I repeat—yet again—that you have nothing to fear from me or anyone else in my band. We demand from you only that you stay put until the ransom is paid."

"And what if it's not?" The question was asked in a tight voice.

Confused by the response, Evan asked, "What if what's not?"

"The ransom, not being paid," the boy said in a tone implying Evan was an idiot—and maybe he was right.

Evander nearly stumbled to a halt. He'd never considered that a possibility and dismissed the question immediately, as it was meant to only provoke him. The baron was a vicious asshole, but the man wouldn't allow anything to happen to his son, even though he wasn't the heir. There was simply no way he'd allow a brigand to get the better of him. A payment of ransom could be hushed up. The killing of his child could not be. The humiliation wasn't something a proud man such as the baron would let happen. He ignored the question and kept going.

They reached the trench and Evan gestured to it. "Take care of your needs. I will give you some privacy, but if you take advantage of it and bolt, I will come get you and make you use a bucket from then on."

Rory glared at him before marching away. Evan kept to his word and used the far end of the trench to relieve himself. It was difficult. His dick hadn't gone limp enough to make pissing easy. And he wasn't going to exacerbate the problem by sneaking peeks at his captive. It was difficult, because the urge to watch him and touch him was strong...stronger than it had been the previous day. If this was what it was like after only one night, how much worse would it get over the next fortnight? It didn't bear thinking about.

When they were both done, he herded the boy back to camp, keeping his hands to himself while watching his captive with an eagle-eye. Being able to see that sweet ass as the boy walked proved difficult, but it was better than laying hands on him again. Evan was relieved to see the old man waiting for them at the pallet with a bowl of water in his hands and a towel slung over his arm. The servant looked as if he'd spent the night in a luxurious bed instead of on Maurice's pallet.

Maxwell gave a shallow bow to his master. "Please sit, sir, and I will refresh you from your night's sleep." He stared a little harder. "Are you feeling well, sir?"

"I'm fine," Rory snapped out. Then he sat cross-legged on the pallet.

"Yes, sir." Maxwell didn't sound convinced, no doubt because his neck was on the chopping block if anything happened to his charge. He knelt beside the boy with a smooth grace and dipped the towel into the water.

Because Evan wanted to stay and watch the servant run that wet cloth over the boy's…everything, he strode away and across the camp to the where Susannah toiled over the cooking fire. She already had a stack of oatcakes on the stump she used as a table, along with some thick, sliced cheese. He grabbed one of each and took a healthy bite.

Susannah smiled at him. "Don't eat so fast. You'll choke one of these days." Although she was younger than he was, she had a motherly way about her.

He took a smaller second bite. "As you say, ma'am."

"And don't talk with your mouth full. Honestly, sometimes I wonder if you were raised in a cave instead of a fancy castle."

Everyone in the band vaguely knew of his origins. At first, he'd tried to blend in, but no amount of trying to alter his speech or dressing down could fool them into thinking he was one of them. They'd known him for the lord he was and also had come to accept that his concern and dedication for the downtrodden was genuine. He no longer felt self-conscious or guilty about how privileged his beginnings had been. None of that mattered now. His life was dedicated to serving others, giving him a purpose he'd never had before. And he held no illusions that if he were captured that his former status would save him from the same punishment as the others. Being sent to the mines, even the women, was the most likely outcome. He didn't so much care about himself, but it hurt to think of someone like Susannah toiling over a cooking pot to feed those who worked hard days in the mines. They wouldn't be kind to her any more than her former masters had been.

Shaking off his morbid thoughts, he polished off his handful of food and reached for more. Susannah was excellent at keeping their stores and making sure everyone knew what their fair share of each meal was. Once he had devoured his oatcakes and cheese, he washed them down with a cup of tea that Susannah always had at the ready. He was contemplating the wisdom of taking his unwilling guest his breakfast when Maxwell approached.

"I will take my master his breakfast now, if you will be so kind as to tell me how much his share is."

Susannah smiled brightly, it being in her nature to be happy now that she wasn't being brutalized, as she gathered two oat cakes, some cheese and a strip of dried venison. "Here you are. I imagine a boy his age has a big appetite."

"Thank you, madam. I will endeavor to get him to eat all of it."

"Wait," Susannah said before the man could take his leave. She held up another oatcake and cheese. "This is for you."

"I thank you, but I will return to eat once my master has finished. If I may?"

Susannah frowned. "Of course. It will be waiting for you when you're ready. No one goes hungry in this camp." With a firm nod, she put down the food and turned back to frying more oatcakes.

Because it was his responsibility to look after his captive, Evan followed the old man as he returned to the pallet. Rory sat in the same place, hugging his knees with his head down. He raised it at his servant's approach, although his gaze homed in on Evan. The boy's cheeks were still flushed, and there was a brightness to his eyes.

Maxwell stooped in front of the boy, breaking Evan's line of sight. "I have your breakfast, sir."

Rory shook his head and went back to staring at the ground. "I'm not hungry."

The old servant tsked. "Come now, sir. Not eating will not do you any good. Don't give them the satisfaction," he added in a low voice meant for the boy's ears only.

Evan had no trouble hearing it even so, and it was on the tip of his tongue to give more reassurance on his safety. Then he changed tactics, believing it would be more effective than endlessly repeating something that no one in Rory's position was going to accept. "Eat your breakfast, boy. Susannah goes to a great deal of trouble keeping us fed, and it's an insult to all those who go hungry every day to turn your noble nose up at simple food."

That did the trick. Rory grabbed the venison and bit off some. As he chewed, he glared at Evander. Uncomfortable with his own guilt, Evan left the boy to his meal and sought out Maurice. His right-hand man was finishing his own breakfast and washing it down with a large mug of mead. A nearby villager kept an apiary and gave them honey when he could. Drinking the fermented beverage for breakfast wasn't Evan's idea of the best way to start the day, but Maurice was a large man with a hard head.

Evan sat on the log beside him. "How was your night?"

Maurice grinned around his mouthful of food. "Quite nice, actually."

"The old man gave you no trouble?"

"Depends on what you think 'trouble' means." He drained his cup. "He slept naked beside me to keep his clothing clean and unwrinkled—or so he told me." Maurice tugged at his crotch. "I woke with the worst case of blue balls."

The statement surprised Evan and reminded him that his nether regions were also discomforted. "You're not saying you're attracted to him?"

"And why shouldn't I be?"

Evan furrowed his brow. "Well…he's old enough to be your father, for one."

Maurice shrugged. "He still has a pretty face and is well-toned under those drab clothes. You know I don't like dipping my wick inside the band. Having someone temporary who's handy has proven to be irresistible to my dick."

"You will not pressure him in any way." One of the most basic rules of his band was that no one could pressure any of the villagers for sexual favors. They did what they did for reasons other than in anticipation of the reward that came from helping those in need. Because they'd never been in this situation before, he thought it worth making it clear that the rules still applied.

Maurice gave him the side-eye. "Don't be insulting. I am not my father."

Evan put his hand on the man's shoulder. "Sorry." It had been unnecessary to give such a reminder. Maurice's mother had been a servant who'd had no choice in his making.

"It's all right. This kidnapping thing is making us all jumpy."

Before Evan could say more, Maxwell hurried over to them. "Sir, I am in need of help."

Evan stood, nervousness swimming in his stomach. "What's wrong?"

"I believe my master is ill."

Now those jitters inside him turned into roils of queasy fear. Had he brought into camp a sickness with his risky scheme? Would all his people fall ill because of his impulsive decision to kidnap this boy? He turned briefly to Maurice. "Fetch Susannah." As he raced to his pallet behind the old servant, every pair of eyes they passed tracked their movement. He saw the worry and questions there yet had nothing more to give them other than a quick smile of reassurance. As they approached Rory, however, all his thoughts and concerns focused on the boy.

The baron's son lay curled on his side under the quilt he'd used for them both during the night. Even before he reached him, Evan could see that his cheeks remained flushed and he shivered once, despite the warmth of day already seeping into the camp. Maxwell kneeled beside his master and ran his hand over strands of sweaty hair. With a little moan, the boy jerked away from the touch.

Trying to convey calm, Evan squatted near the end of the pallet. "What ails you, boy?" When his question was met with another moan, he looked at Maxwell. "Was there a sickness at the castle before you left?"

"No." The servant's expression was grim, and there was something more showing in it…anger.

"Then what is the matter with him? Does he have a fever?" He wished Susannah would hurry up. She was an accomplished herbalist and healer, so much so that she often made rounds to the villages to offer her help.

"Yes," was Maxwell's simple reply. "I noticed he was warm when I bathed him and when he didn't eat…"

A cough suddenly racked Rory. Instead of moving away to avoid the bad vapors, the servant tried to take the boy by his shoulders to raise his chest. Small as he was, the baron's son was nevertheless too much for the nearly as small and thin old man to handle.

"Here… I'll help him." Evan moved to the other side of the boy and lifting him by the armpits, placed him against his chest. His leather vest and the tunic under it did nothing to block the heat emanating from his captive. And it was a testament to how badly the boy felt that he didn't struggle against the hold, merely lay limp against him. *How has he gotten so ill so quickly?* The obvious answer was that it hadn't happened fast. The illness had been brewing overnight, but in his haste to keep the boy at a distance, he'd missed the signs that he was sick. And of course, the mulish brat had said nothing, undoubtedly because he didn't want to show weakness to his enemy.

As another cough overtook the boy, Evan held on to him while he bent over from the force of it. He could feel the vibration against his own chest. Still, it didn't sound too deep. Perhaps the sickness wasn't much more than a summer cold. That could turn nasty, he knew, except he was determined not to allow that to happen. Relief coursed through him as Susannah approached, her satchel slung over her shoulder and a cup cradled between her hands.

Passing the cup to Maxwell, she nudge him aside to take his place. "What have we here?" Her gentle tone made even the toughest of men relax. With light touches to his brow, she tested the strength of Rory's fever, then picked up his wrist to feel his life pulse. "Not too bad. I have something to bring your temperature down and ease that cough." She took the cup from Maxwell's hands and pressed it against Rory's lips. "Come now. It's nothing to fear, only some willow bark, marshmallow root and honey. It doesn't taste too bad, and it will make you feel much better."

When Rory continued to refuse to drink, Evan held out his hand. "Give it to me." With only a slight hesitation and a warning in her eyes, the woman did as he said. Evan held Rory by the jaw with one hand while pressing the cup to his lips. "Drink. I will not have you exposing my people to sickness any more than you already have." He hadn't meant to sound so stern, yet it did the trick.

On a shudder, Rory opened his mouth and sipped at the medicine. Apparently finding it palatable, he swallowed more down quickly until the cup was empty. Then panting from the effort, he lolled his head on Evan's chest, proof that the lad must feel very sick indeed. That was the only reason why he would make himself to so vulnerable to his enemy. He coughed again, but this time it had less force. Handing the cup back to Susannah, Evan resigned himself to sit for a long while with his captive sprawled against him. It wasn't hard. The lad weighed practically nothing. He hadn't realized how thin and delicate the boy was just by looking at him or during the brief time he'd held him at the moment of capture. Now that he had him in his arms, he could tell that he needed some fattening up—and care. Great care. His protective instincts kicked in like a mule. Grabbing the quilt, he tucked it all around Rory and held him firmly in his arms.

Maxwell stared at him with an unreadable expression before standing. "I'll fetch some cool water to bathe his brow. If there is any to be had," he added. "The water warming by the cooking fire will not do."

Evan gestured with his jaw toward Maurice, who lingered nearby. "He'll escort you to the stream we get our fresh water from. As close to the mountains as we are, the water is practically frigid."

After sketching a short bow, the man picked up the bowl he'd used for the bathing water and walked over to Maurice, then dutifully followed him with only one backward glance at his master. Evan gave him a quick, reassuring smile, although he knew the man had no reason to trust him with his young charge. Still, Evan was determined that no matter how unforgiveable his actions had been so far, he wasn't going to give either the boy or his servant reason to fear that he was a monster. And fortunately, his wayward dick agreed with him. Despite having the alluring ass snuggled between his legs, he felt not a glimmer of arousal. All his attention was focused on Rory's breathing and the small shudders that occasionally racked his body. Both were easing, thank the gods. Susannah's concoctions worked well and quickly.

By the time Maxwell returned, Evan was sure Rory had fallen asleep. He reluctantly laid him gently onto the pallet so that the servant could tend to him properly. The boy didn't stir and only murmured a little as the old man began to bathe his brow with a wet cloth. His shiny, pink lips moved without sound as little, puffy coughs passed them. Finally, he settled altogether, his face smoothed out in a deep, peaceful slumber. Maxwell stared down at the boy for a few seconds before moving away to dump the water on the ground.

Evan followed him, one eye still on the boy. "What does he have? You say there was no sickness brewing within the castle, but clearly he was unwell when he started his journey."

The old man stared at the ground. "I could tell he was out of sorts. That's not unusual, as I'm sure you've noticed yourself."

Evan raised an eyebrow. "Well, I'm not seeing the lad under the best of circumstances. He has a right to be snippy with me."

Maxwell's lips quirked up. "A fair point." He turned pensive. "For all that, he's not prone to showing physical weakness."

"And why not?" Having been raised as Rory had, he knew that one of the privileges of being of the nobility was access to the best of care when sickness came.

The old man gave him a measured look before responding with a question. "Do prey animals exhibit signs of disease before succumbing to it?"

Evan answered without considering what the point was. "Not usually. They instinctively know not to show weakness around predators. It makes them an easy target." As soon as the last word had left his mouth, understanding came. He took a step toward the old man, reining in a sudden fury. "Who does he hide this from...his father?" *Obviously.* Why would a man known to be so vicious toward those under his control be any different with his own child?

Maxwell nodded grimly. "Yes, and his two older brothers. They are cut from the same cloth as the baron."

"But Rory isn't?"

"No. Nor is he much like the late baroness. For all that she kept him close, she was little better than her husband—selfish, greedy and with a good measure of vanity. She was a beautiful woman and resented being given to a man who was not well-formed."

"And Rory must take after her in his looks, because I've seen the baron and he has the face of a toad. Plus, his coloring is much darker." He could still picture the ruddy-faced man with graying black hair. He'd only seen him the once and hadn't bothered to stare too long at him. Yet, his image was clear enough. His dark eyes had been lit with fury at some poor peasant who'd dared to question the need for such high taxes. The rings on his thick fingers had sparkled in the sunlight as he'd whipped his crop at the man. That had been the moment for him that had hardened his nascent idea of how he might help those under the bastard's yoke.

The servant averted his gaze. "Not really, no. He looks quite different from the rest of his entire family on both sides."

Evan let that unexpected response slide. Learning about the boy's life story wasn't the point. "How did he become sick if there was nothing brewing within the castle? Did he frequent a brothel or something before leaving?"

"Hardly." The man's tone was dismissive. Then it was as if he deflated under Evan's gaze. "I expect he caught a chill a few days ago after he…he was forced to swim back and forth within the lake. Like your stream, the water is quite chilly, no matter the season."

Evan's gut tightened because he knew he wasn't going to like the answer to his next question. "Why?"

"He was being disciplined by the baron for some infraction." The man shook his head. "It's hard to know what will or did offend the man. It is enough that he deems it worthy to mete out the punishment." He heaved a sigh and closed his eyes. "Afterward, he made the boy stand naked and wet in the courtyard. He kept him there well into the night. I was finally allowed to bring him in and put him in a hot bath when the usual revels ended. I thought he was fine. Certainly, he dismissed any of my concerns. That event has to be the cause of this. I can think of no other reason for his taking ill. And he's usually quite healthy, all things considered," he added with a sigh.

Somehow, Evan knew the boy well enough to have no trouble picturing him standing naked, shivering and miserable while his father's soldiers undoubtedly mocked him for it. He knew that the denizens of a keep took their cues from the lord. And although he'd been raised in a place where his parents established rules for fairness and compassion both by word and deed, others of their status didn't share that vision of the proper way to treat people. Except for Maxwell, there was probably no one else at the castle who would dare show kindness and concern to the boy under those circumstances. "Does he not trust you at least to see his weaknesses?"

Maxwell looked at him with a profound sadness clearly showing in his expression. "He trusts no one."

Chapter Four

Rory woke from a fitful sleep of strange dreams. They weren't exactly nightmares, although frightening animals had chased him through dark woods. And his heart had been pounding and his breath labored, but there had also been a sense of security. Someone had shadowed him through his trek. His mind wouldn't allow him to see who, yet he'd known that this was his protector, a man who would stick by his side, shielding him from the danger. As he shook off his sleep, he felt sticky and uncomfortable, although not from lingering images of what his mind had conjured. He was sick. He'd known first thing in the morning when he'd opened his eyes to see his captor scrutinizing him. Long, horrible years of experience allowed him to hide his pounding head and scratchy throat. But the fever had climbed quickly, and soon it had become impossible to pretend he was well. Maxwell, in particular, was too adept at reading him.

Still, he felt better and remembered how the brigand had forced him to drink some warm brew that had been surprisingly sweet. The medicine was working, and for that he was grateful, although no less wary. He couldn't afford to show weakness in front of these people—or rather no more than he already had. Kindness could be shown in one instance, then turn quickly into a meanness that was all the worse for what had preceded it. He was too clever to fall into that trap. Part of him wondered if it wouldn't be better to simply succumb to the illness. That would be easier for everyone. But no, if his mother had given him anything of worth, it had been a strong sense of self-preservation.

As he lay on his side working up the energy to open his eyes, a cough overtook him and there was simply no way to stifle it.

Strong, yet gentle, hands cupped his shoulders. "Easy now. I have you."

Those three words sounded odd to his suspicious ears, but the rest of him had no trouble accepting them as genuine kindness. And he knew the voice, of course. It wasn't the grimly determined Maxwell who helped him now. It was the brigand. *Evander. Evan.* Rory didn't dare use either name out loud. The man wasn't his friend. He was strong, however, and when he lifted Rory to lie against his broad, hard chest, he didn't resist, nor did he fight drinking more of the medicine. If nothing else, he knew his captor needed to keep him alive in the hopes of exchanging him for the ransom. *If only he knew.* Rory nearly smiled, a grim sort of humor at the knowledge of how Evan would soon learn that he'd wasted his time and effort.

At the moment, however, Rory knew that life meant hope, so he drank the warm, sweet liquid down without complaint. When he was finished, he felt as if he'd sprinted through the woods and was too weak to mind how he sprawled in Evan's lap. He wasn't worried, either, that he'd feel how much the man obviously wanted him. He'd seen that hungry look in a man's eye many times since even before he'd entered into manhood. It chilled him to the bone, but he always acted indifferent, as if he had no clue what was going on. Evan wanted him, he was sure of it, and if he were clever, perhaps he could seduce the man into wanting to keep him, no matter the payment of the ransom. The thought of a man touching him in that way made him cringe. He'd seen for himself how men wielded that thing between their legs that they were so proud of. It was a brutal and painful business, and he wasn't sure he could survive such treatment. Death might be the better of that bargain. Except he didn't feel any hardness pressed against him. If Evan was aroused, his clothing hid it well. Still, Rory tried to pull away.

Evan held him in place with a firm hug of one arm. "Rest, my lord. Your fever broke once in your sleep, but it's come back again."

As another cough consumed him, Rory briefly thought that it would take no effort to simply fall on his face. But he didn't fight the hold as he had little strength. So he wielded his tongue instead. "You are obviously of an educated class, if not the nobility itself. How is it you don't know that the sons of a baron are not lords? At best, I am the Honorable Rory Finley, not that it means much to anyone," he added in a mutter. His energy was already flagging with such little effort having been expended.

The brigand had the temerity to chuckle. "I am aware of the title traditions, although I frankly find the whole thing absurd. How about I simply call you Rory?

Do you feel up to eating? Susannah has made a broth that should go down easily."

Thrown off balance by hearing his name uttered in the brigand's smooth, deep voice, he didn't answer the second question immediately. He took stock of how his stomach felt, and although he couldn't claim to be hungry, broth sounded appealing. "Yes, please." He wasn't sure the man holding him would take him to mean applying to both questions or not, but he responded to it as about the food. "I think I can stomach something simple like that."

"Excellent. Lie down again on your side, and I'll fetch a bowl."

The moment Rory was laid down on the pallet, he perversely missed the warmth of Evan's hold. "Maxwell can do that." It was disconcerting to enjoy the man's touch, and he wanted to put distance between them. Getting comfortable was a bad idea. He was a prisoner, after all, and he needed to keep that horrible truth in mind.

"Your manservant is busy helping Susannah with the evening meal. He was quite worried about you but has graciously allowed me to tend over you. He's devoted to you. You might take more care in how you speak with him."

Rory didn't respond, and the man didn't wait around for one. How could he explain, even if he wanted to, his feelings for the man who had been both complicit in his misery and protective of him once his mother had died? His life didn't fit neatly into some role that society would understand or appreciate. Some might pity him, but mostly he'd lived with a scorn that had made him want to run away and hide. Maxwell was a place of safety, to be sure. He was also a handy person to vent his spleen with because there was no one else. Thinking of his complicated relationship with the old man made his headache come back, so he lay on his side with his eyes closed until Evan returned.

"Here we are." The man's cheerful tone should have been grating.

The fact that it wasn't put Rory's back up, so he frowned as Evan helped him sit and resisted when the guy pulled him into the V of his legs once more. "I can sit on my own."

"Oh, I beg your pardon." Evan let go of him, then caught him with one hand when Rory started to fall over. "Not everything has to be a minor war, Rory."

"So you say." Because he'd learned to pick his battles, he gave in to what he wanted anyway by leaning against Evan's strength. And when the bowl of broth was placed against his lips, he found that he was hungry after all. He sipped the warm liquid slowly. "Your woman is an excellent cook," he said when half the bowl had been consumed.

"Yes she is, although she is not mine. No one is here. I refer to everyone around us as 'my band', 'my men', 'my people', but they aren't. Not really. They belong to themselves and follow me willingly. It's humbling and quite often frightening, if I'm to be honest."

Rory took another sip. The fact that the man confided in him was surprising and somehow as warming as the broth. "I've known men as powerful and commanding as you obviously are. To confess to any doubt or weakness is a mistake. It's not safe to do so."

The man barked out a laugh as he tipped the bowl so that Rory could drain it. "Only the truly weak-minded worry about such things. I know the measure of my worth, but I'm still concerned that I will do these people harm."

"Then why take up this life? Brigands often end up dangling from a rope or losing their heads—at best, working themselves to any early death in the mines." The mere thought of such a fate for this man should have been welcome. Somehow it wasn't. "If you give this folly up now, you can disappear into these woods and make a new life for yourself. The world is a big place, or so I hear. You could go far away where no one would know you or what you did."

"Would that it were so simple." Putting down the bowl, Evan repositioned Rory so that his head lay on the man's lap, then tucked the quilt around him. "Do you have any idea what life is like for all the peasants living on your father's land?"

"I know the baron is a harsh man."

"And greedy."

"That, too. He loves to live large and in great comfort. My mother was the same before her death."

"All of which requires coin—lots of it."

"I suppose it does. I've never had any. Everything I have was given to me." *And a stingy amount, as well, just enough to give the illusion that the baron's youngest son was a nobleman.* "I know nothing about how the baron makes his wealth."

"Through breaking the backs of those who toil his land and craft what is needed for living." As the man spoke his harsh words, he petted Rory's head. Not since his mother had anyone soothed him in such a way, and even then, her touch had been harsher than this. "From the farmers to the brewers and the huntsman to the weavers, everyone must pay your father taxes that leave them barely enough to survive on. Many don't during the harsh winter months."

Rory frowned at the information. He knew others suffered at the baron's hand. He'd seen plenty of it in the castle. It had never occurred to him how those in the surrounding area might be affected by the man's evil nature. "I know nothing about such matters. He doesn't confide in me, and I would never dare ask, because it's none of my business. I'm not his heir or even his spare. Are you saying that you rob people to help others?" That seemed unlikely. Brigands were criminals, not saviors.

"That is exactly what we do. It's little enough, and our success means that fewer wealthy people take this route if they can avoid it. We have taken to lying in wait on other, smaller roads, but it takes time to position ourselves, and we never know if it will be a day for a traveler to pass by. Most days, they don't. We have less coin to distribute these days."

Understanding dawned. "You kidnapped me to get more money to make up for that shortfall."

Evan didn't answer right away. "Yes. It's not well done of me, and you have every right to hate me for it. I simply don't know what else to do."

He almost said *I don't hate you,* but that would be foolish. Whatever else this man was, he held Rory's life in his hands, and he was unlikely to view him as one of the downtrodden. When no ransom arrived, he wouldn't want an extra and utterly useless mouth to feed, either. "I can't help you in any of this. I have no power or knowledge that could aid you in your goal, even if I wanted to."

"I understand." The man sat quietly for a while, his fingers never leaving Rory's head. "Are you comfortable?"

Rory surprised himself by saying, "Yes."

"Then sleep some more. Susannah says it's the best medicine, and you needn't worry while you do so. I'm here to take care of you."

That statement shouldn't have reassured him, yet somehow it did. Closing his eyes, he allowed himself to drift off.

* * * *

Evan was known for being calm, cool and collected. His reputation would seem unfounded to anyone watching him now. As they waited for their contacts from the villages to arrive, he kept walking in tight circles and staring over his shoulder. It wasn't an ambush he worried about. No, his attention kept turning in the direction of where the camp lay. More precisely, he was picturing Rory there, then wondering how he was and wishing he hadn't had to leave him. He told himself that it was merely because keeping the boy from escaping was his responsibility. That wasn't the real reason. Maurice was there to keep an eye out, and Rory had only just recovered from what had mercifully amounted to a mild and short illness. His fever had been gone for two days and his coughing had all but disappeared. Evan wasn't needed there. It was important, though, for him to show his face in particular when handing over their spoils to those in need. The villagers counted on his ability to lead the band. It would make them nervous if he didn't show up.

Nemo stepped in front of him. "This pacing of yours is driving me crazy. You're never antsy like this. I can only assume it's the boy you worry about." They snorted. "Or do you miss having him in your lap while you pet him like a dog?"

Evan scowled. "Don't be ridiculous. I'm merely concerned that our very valuable captive needs to be returned in good health. Tending to him was my job, obviously."

"*Obviously*. It's not as if he had a servant to care for him. Oh wait... Yes, he did." Nemo leaned in closer so that the others perched around them as lookouts couldn't see or hear. "You're not fooling anyone, Evan. Even a celibate like Manfred can see that you want the boy."

Evan waved away that observation, true as it was. "Who wouldn't be attracted to such a pretty piece. He's not mine to play with, however. He will be sent back to the baron in exactly the same condition in which we found him."

"That day can't come too soon. It's unnerving to have those two outsiders living among us, and we'll have to move camp once they're gone in case they have a better sense of direction than we think they do."

"I *know*." Evan couldn't keep the testiness out of his voice. "It's past time for doing so anyway. We've been in the same spot for too long." He did understand the need for caution, but he also couldn't imagine Rory or his manservant leading the baron's soldiers to them. Not only did he believe they had no ability to navigate the thick woods, but he also had the feeling that neither the boy nor the man thought much about their liege lord and wouldn't be inclined to help him. *Keep telling yourself that.* It was probably no more than fanciful thinking, a misinterpretation of how Rory had stopped fighting him over every little thing. The boy had been sick, and Evan had brought him comfort and healing. It was no more than a sense of gratitude, if the boy felt anything kind toward him at all. Once he was back in the safety of his father's domain, the lad would regain his fury over being kidnapped.

One of their sentries perched in a tree called out the signal that meant the villagers' representatives approached.

Pushing thought of Rory aside, Evan stepped into the small clearing that served as one of their rotating places to meet up. Two men, one tall and lean and one short and broad, approached. The shorter one was grizzled with age. The other was younger than Evan, a man who had gained unusual status within his village in only a few years. It had been he who had seen the benefit of trusting Evan and his band when others had been leery. He'd spent countless days going from village to village, stating his case. Without his help, Evan might never have convinced the baron's peasants to trust him and take the money he stole on their behalf.

Evan stepped forward and offered his hand to the younger man. "Henry, it's good to see you. And John." He shook the older man's hand in turn. "How fare your crops this season?"

"Passable," John replied. "The harvest should be good this year, then the tax collector will take a big chunk of it and the coin it brings at the market, as always."

Evan grinned. "And we'll steal it back from him. We've tracked his alternate route and will be positioned there when the time is ripe." Turning to Nemo, he held out his hand. They dropped the purse they'd taken off Rory's coachman into his palm. Evan tossed it to Henry. "Compliments of the baron. It comes directly from a coach carrying his son."

John rubbed his chin. "We heard about it. There's been talk of little else, albeit in hushed tones. Bad business, Evan. Very bad."

He grimaced. "I understand your point. We didn't take the boy with a light heart. It's simply that you need more than we've collected so far, and if we're wrong about ambushing the tax collector, you'll need a cushion of coin to get through the winter."

"We don't question your decisions, Evan," Henry interjected. "You have been too true to us for that. We trust your judgment...but in this, I believe you have miscalculated. This whole business isn't going to end the way you expect it to."

Evan felt a spike of nerves. "What do you mean? We have the baron's *son*. There is a risk of entrapment, yes. We've planned for an ambush to be waiting when we rendezvous for the ransom. The fucker has to save face by at least trying to take us down. But we've asked for a modest amount by the baron's standard of living to get his boy back unharmed. He won't want for anything for giving it up."

"That's just the thing." Henry frowned. "I don't think the baron intends to pay for his release at all. Let me explain," he hastily added when Evan took a step toward him. His alarm must have showed clearly on his face. "I have a cousin who works in the castle, as you know. The baron has been keeping the news of his son's kidnapping quiet as much as possible. But Daphne heard him discussing it with his trusted advisors as she served them, and the baron has said he won't pay anything for the 'little bastard', as he called him. He doesn't care what happens and actually laughed about how you'll do him a favor by slitting the lad's throat."

Evan's stomach dropped, and he held out his hand to ward off any comment from Nemo. He turned to pace once more, trying to absorb this unexpected weakness in his plan. Henry, or rather his cousin, had to have heard wrong. How could even a man as cruel and selfish as the baron leave his child to twist in the wind? Surely pride alone dictated that he rescue his son by paying the ransom. Not doing so gave the impression that Evander and his band ruled these woods and that the baron was impotent to stop it. No ruler could tolerate that sort of public humiliation. And yet, as Henry's tale settled into his mind, he realized that not only was it true, but that he wasn't surprised by it. His captives had left verbal crumbs for him to follow to this very place.

He whirled to face the village man. "You're sure of this?"

"My cousin is, and she's of an age and little beauty where men such as the baron and his cronies don't notice her. She's like a stick of furniture, and they speak freely when she's serving them. She knows the boy, as well, obviously, and says he gets rough treatment from his father and older brothers. And since his mother's death, he's secluded most of the time in his room with only an old manservant for company. I don't think the baron's words were bluster, Evan. No ransom will be paid, then what will you do with the boy?"

"He's a liability," John added. "Best to send him on his way and hope he gets lost in the forest forever. If you don't, he may cause trouble for all of us."

"I will do no such thing!" At Nemo's raised eyebrows, he tempered his tone. "It would be kinder to slit the boy's throat than leave him to starve or be torn apart and eaten by a pack of wolves. And I'm not doing that, either. He's my problem," he added with a firm nod. "I was the one to hatch this scheme, and I will find a solution that won't jeopardize any of us. You have my word on that."

Henry nodded back. "We trust you, Evan. Don't we, John?"

"Aye." The old man didn't seem entirely convinced. "They say the lad's a bit peevish in nature, so I'm sure you're going to want to rid yourself of him quickly, somehow."

"Yes," Evan agreed. "He's quite the brat, and I'm beginning to understand why." He almost said 'spoiled' but if what the observant Daphne had said were true, that word didn't fit at all. "Safe journeys, and I hope that bit of coin will be helpful."

Henry tossed the bag in his palm before tucking it away in his satchel. "It always is." The man and John raised their hands in farewell and disappeared into the trees the way they'd come.

Nemo crossed their arms. "So, what are we to do now? I suppose we should wait to make sure no one returns with the ransom at the appointed time. But I know Daphne some, and she's a sensible woman. She wouldn't pass on idle gossip. The boy is useless to us, I'll wager."

Evan rubbed his chin, his mind reeling with the puzzle of what to do with Rory. "I'm certain she's right. I never considered this possibility." *Damn!*

Nemo put their hand on his arm. "Don't kick yourself over this, Evan. No one could have predicted that we'd kidnap someone whose family didn't care to ransom them back. It certainly didn't occur to me that the baron's son would prove to be a millstone instead of a golden opportunity. I know you're not going to kill him," they added with a wry grin.

"No, I certainly will not. The obvious next step is to take him and his servant back to the road. I'm sure someone will help them at the nearest village. And as we discussed, we were going to move our camp afterward anyway to be sure they couldn't lead soldiers to it. This is simply an annoyance. We'll try again after we set up our new camp, and hopefully we'll have better luck next time."

Nemo snorted. "Sure, let's double down on the crazy idea that led us to this situation in the first place. At least you didn't say you were going to keep him. That's something." Signaling the others to leave, they headed back.

Evan didn't follow right away. He stood thinking about how he'd almost said that very thing—*keep him.*

Chapter Five

Rory had to act fast if he was going to escape. He'd been given the gift of Evan leaving the camp to pass along the money he'd taken during the kidnapping. He wasn't sure why the man had to do it personally, but he wasn't going to let the opportunity pass. Although he had a few days yet before the brigand would learn that no ransom was going to be paid, he saw no reason to wait for that moment. Doing so would be like baring his throat to be slit like an animal to be slaughtered. As bad as his life was, he wasn't ready to throw it away. And he was lucky that his illness had passed. He was relatively clean, rested and well-fed. There would never be a better time for him to try his luck at running away into the forest.

He wrapped the bit of food he'd managed to squirrel away with each meal over the last few days in the scrap of cloth Maxwell used to wash him. Then he tucked it under his tunic and secured it by cinching it tightly with his belt. He'd lost some weight with his sickness, so the package wasn't obvious. A quick glance around confirmed that no one was paying him any mind. Because Evan had made him his personal responsibility, none of the brigands were in the habit of checking up on him. And no one other than Maxwell ever came near him, except for Susannah when he'd needed her medicinals. He didn't need her anymore, so she tended her cooking fire at the far end of the camp. She hadn't looked in his direction all day.

As for Maxwell, he was occupied with the big, ugly brute that he'd taken an interest in. The two of them sat talking about the gods knew what. Both were engrossed with each other and not looking at him, either. Maxwell would try to stop him, he was sure it, from some misguided expectation that Rory wouldn't be harmed. The old man had dropped lots of hints about his feelings, about how kind the brigands were and wasn't it a relief to know they didn't have sneak around and go unnoticed all the time? Sure, in many ways there was more freedom in being a captive here than being in the castle. That didn't mean there was no danger. These people simply prided themselves on being better than the nobility who preyed on them…kinder, except that veneer would fall off as soon as they learned that they had made a mistake in taking him. Maxwell would probably be fine. He was, for all intents and purposes, one of them, and he had skills to pull his weight. There was no need for him to risk his life running away. He'd be grateful to Rory in the end for leaving him behind.

Now is the time.

His heart pounded with mounting fear. This would not be an easy journey. There were a great many dangers in these woods. He didn't need to believe anything Evan said to understand that. Each night, he heard them—howling, growling and screeching at one another. Unarmed as he was, he would be no match for their claws and fangs. He would have to rely on his wits to survive, although he knew better than anyone that he didn't have much of those, either. The baron hadn't afforded him any amount of training as a soldier, and while there was much to be learned from books, nothing he'd ever read taught him how to survive in the wild.

There was no hope for it. If death was coming for him, he'd rather die trying to live than stay and cower as Evan made him pay for the baron's refusal to ransom him back. Part of him was just as naïve as Maxwell was being. He couldn't imagine the man who had nursed him with such tender care could kill him. But that was wishful thinking. Evan had made him well to preserve his value. That was all. Reading any motive behind it more than that was folly. And the man had committed himself to leading his men and helping the peasants. Rory's fate was sealed by that devotion. Anything other than killing his hostage would be too risky. He could only hope that Maxwell, one of the downtrodden, would not only be spared but maybe also given some coin and the opportunity to start his life anew somewhere else. The old man deserved some kind of benefit for his loyal service, even if Rory couldn't forgive him for the role he'd played in his mother's selfish actions.

He rose slowly from the pallet, not giving anyone a reason to notice him. With small, quiet steps, he slipped behind a nearby tree. This was the way to the privy. If someone spotted him, that was the answer he was going to give. He walked backward, staring at the camp, keeping an eye out for Maxwell or others who might come his way. No one did, and when he couldn't see the others anymore, he turned and ran. There was nowhere he was trying to go. He only wanted to get as far away as possible, and assuming Evan would look for him heading toward the road, he went in a direction that he believed would take him farther into the forest. He wasn't sure of his bearings, but he could remember the direction of how he'd entered the camp. It was simply a matter of going in the opposite way of that. It didn't take long before the sounds of the camp had faded completely. All that was around him were those things that belonged naturally in these woods. Knowing that he wasn't one of them, he prayed he would be left alone.

* * * *

Evan knew something was terribly wrong the moment he stepped foot into the camp. Everyone was clustered in a tight circle with voices raised. His stomach dropped when he gazed toward his pallet and saw that it was empty. *Rory.* He raced to his people and pushed his way into the center where Manfred stood arguing with Maurice. Beside them, Maxwell wrung his hands but said nothing. His eyes went wide as he spied Evan, although there was something like relief that flashed across his face instead of the usual wariness.

"What's going on?" Evan's shout caused a sudden silence, as he'd intended. "Where's Rory?" He tried not to sound like a man on the verge of violence, but it was hard to hold back his fury…and his fear. He knew the answer before it was given, and the only thing he really cared about was whether anyone had seen the direction the boy had left in.

"The boy has fled, Evan," Maurice said with a grimace.

"No shit. How did it happen and when? You were supposed to be watching him." He and Maurice had had their differences from time-to-time but never had he wanted to plow his fist into the man's homely face the way he did now.

Maurice looked ashamed. "I know…and I'm sorry. I didn't think I needed to sit on him. I wasn't far away, and I kept glancing in his direction. He was there every time…until he wasn't," he said lamely.

"The fault is mine." This from Maxwell. The old man held his chin high as he elaborated. "Watching my master is my duty, and not only did I neglect that, I also distracted Maurice from the task you set for him. If anything happens to that boy, I will never forgive myself. I should have anticipated that he would leave without saying anything to me."

Evan stared at the man. "You both knew there would be no ransom, didn't you?"

The others gasped at the news, but Maxwell didn't seem surprised at the question. "Yes, we did."

He leaned into the man. "I will hear the whole of it once the boy is back safely. Now, where was he when he was last seen?"

"On your pallet, of course," Manfred answered. "We've all been keeping our distance, given how difficult he can be. We thought it your bed to lie in, but it is to our eternal shame that we didn't treat the boy better."

"There will be time enough for guilt. Come on." Evan stalked over to his pallet to pick up the trail. It was easily done. The boy may have been clever enough to leave camp without being seen or heard, but he had no skill at covering his tracks. Evan lifted his hand to ward the others off. "I will go after him alone. Spooked as he is, being descended upon by a group of us will only make him run faster instead of waiting to hear me out and perhaps coming back of his own volition. Besides, I don't like leaving the camp unattended by warriors. There should be no particular concern, except this whole situation has worried me. The idea that the baron will simply forget about his son doesn't sit well with me, either. Who knows what the man is really planning? I will feel better if you two are here in particular," he added with a nod at Maurice and Nemo.

Maurice stepped forward. "Don't worry about us, Evan. Find the boy."

With that reassurance ringing in his ears, Evan began to track his quarry. It took no great effort to do so. The boy's small, booted feet left impressions on the muddy parts of the ground and broken stalks of fronds were like arrows pointing the right direction. Rory was clearly heading farther into the forest—a smart move, but also one that increased Evan's worry. There were many dangers lurking about, and animals lying in wait for a tasty morsel such as the boy was only one of them. He picked up his pace, his long legs eating up more distance than Rory could. If he were lucky, he would catch up to him soon, before the night started to fall and blinded them both with darkness.

* * * *

Rory followed the sound of rushing water and was happy to see a fast-moving stream. He knew there was a water source near the camp, perhaps part of this one. It looked cool and inviting, but it wasn't thirst that he needed to slake that was the issue. If he followed it one way, it led up, and he feared the terrain would become too rocky for him to traverse. And he was sure that if he went in the opposite direction, it would circle him back to the camp. If he wanted to lose himself deep within the woods, he needed to go across. As he stood by the bank, he gauged the level of the fast-moving water and studied its rocky bottom. He judged he could keep his footing, except that his boots and trousers up to his knees would get soaking wet. With night descending, he couldn't afford to get chilled in wet clothes. There really was only one thing to do.

Sitting on a nearby boulder, he took everything off. There was no point in risking getting his tunic wet, either. It wasn't too chilly yet, and he was used to being a little cold anyway. It was a favorite punishment of the baron to stand him naked where everyone could see. He enjoyed Rory's humiliation, especially when his soldiers leered openly at him and called out lewd suggestions. Discomfort was a constant companion, so this trek across a cold stream wasn't much of an obstacle. He bundled up his clothing as best he could and tucked it and his boots under one arm. The first step into the water confirmed that it ran from a nearby mountain range, its icy cold making him hiss. He ignored it and forced himself to walk determinedly past the bank, although he had to be careful or he'd lose his footing on the slippery bottom.

"Rory!"

The sound of his name being hollered in that familiar voice made him jump. He started to slip and struggled to remain upright. As he did so, he looked over his shoulder to confirm that Evan had found him. The sight of the man racing toward him with a furious look made him want to cry in frustration. But he was determined to make his escape and abandoned his effort to be careful. He'd taken no more than two hurried steps before his foot skidded against a rock. For a few seconds, he teetered this way and that, trying to regain his balance. Nevertheless, he ended up splashing down on his ass, his arms flailing and his clothing and boots flying out and into the rushing water. He couldn't hold back a cry and flinched as all except the top of his head became wet. He struggled to gain purchase on the stream's bed, even as he watched helplessly while his clothing was washed away. To make matters worse, the wind started to whip around him.

Evan stripped off his vest and tunic. "*Rory*. Stay put. I'm coming for you."

Rory wanted to scream at the man to go away and leave him alone, but he couldn't find his feet, and the rocks were rough against his ass. Tears started to streak down his cheeks, one of the few places not already wet. He hated showing the weakness, but he simply wasn't suited to surviving in the wild. *What did I expect? I'm useless.*

Evan arrived with admirable agility and scooped him up as if he were a guppy in a pond. He hoisted Rory against his bare chest, and the warmth of the brigand's skin seeped into him instantly. He curled into the embrace, humiliated yet in dire need of the comfort. Evan placed him on the very boulder he'd used in order to strip. Then he used fistfuls of nearby moss to rub his torso dry before tucking Rory into his tunic. Of course, the garment was almost like a dress on him, but he hunched into its warmth, all sense of pride gone.

"Stay here. I'll see what I can do about rescuing your clothes." Evan didn't sound nearly as mad as he must be. The man acted as if this were nothing more than an ordinary chore.

Rory looked away, wishing he were somewhere else—somewhere warm and quiet, a place to lick his wounds in private. He looked mournfully down at his sogging wet boots when Evan tossed them beside the rock.

"Your clothing is lost, I'm afraid. The stream is deceptively fast and dangerous up here. What were you thinking trying to cross it? No, don't answer that," he added immediately. "You wanted to escape and across the stream was your only chance for that."

Rory closed his eyes a moment. "Why did you come after me?" He was so damn weary that he blurted out the very thing he'd been hiding since his kidnapping. "It was pointless for you to do so. The baron won't pay the ransom." He flashed Evan a look of anger. "You've wasted your time and effort. You should have let me run away. Then you'd be free of the burden of dispatching me yourself." He stared at the ground, expecting a knife across his throat at any moment. In truth, he almost welcomed it.

Instead, Evan stood there, silent. His gaze bore a hole into Rory. Finally, he said, "I know…about the ransom, I mean. My contacts in the villages told me that word came through the servants at the castle that the baron has washed his hands of you. Maxwell confirmed that he knew it all along, as did you. The question is…why? Why won't he pay to get you back?"

Rory laughed mirthlessly. "Does it really matter? Isn't it enough that he can and has?"

"Not to me. You may be a third son, but surely a man like him wants as much of his progeny walking about as possible. Life is precarious. Your older brothers could succumb to illness or violence. It's not unheard of for a child farther down the family tree to become a nobleman's heir. How is it that he'd let a son of his to be lost to him?"

Raising his gaze, Rory told the secret that he'd guarded inside him for many years. "The answer to that question is easy, as it happens. Because I'm not his son."

* * * *

Rory huddled by the fire Evan had started, the man's tunic serving as both blanket and clothing. The tunic was made of soft wool and smelled musky like Evan. It was a purely masculine scent, and, far from being unpleasant, it made Rory feel ridiculously safe. The man himself wore only his leather vest over his chest, leaving a lot of skin showing. For the first time, he could see the sinewy muscles that gave the brigand his strength. He'd caught a couple of fish, dug up some tubers and even picked berries. It was all being fashioned into a simple, yet welcome feast. Rory tried not to feel like a calf being fatted for slaughter—a ridiculous thought. If Evan had wanted him dead, he'd be dead. The question now was what did he intend to do with him?

As Evan handed him some food laid out on a piece of bark, Rory figured he may as well just ask. "What are you going to do with me?" He scooped up some fish with his fingers and popped it into his mouth. Gods, he was suddenly ravenous and hurried to eat more. He didn't dare look at Evan.

The man sighed. "Well, that's a question. I don't have a ready answer. Tell me why you believe you're not the baron's son."

Rory swallowed his mouthful. "It's not a belief but a fact. Everyone at the castle suspects but no one says it out loud, of course. My father—the man who made me, rather—is someone else, a visiting young knight, apparently."

"Which knight and how do you know about him?"

Rory shrugged. "I don't know his name. My mother took him to bed, and if she ever bothered to learn his name, she never told me."

Evan stared at him wide-eyed. "But she did tell you, her son, that she'd lain with another man to conceive you?" He shook his head and shoved food into his mouth. "What a world this is."

"She might not have ever confessed it to me, but she was sick, dying, when I was nine. She called me to her bed and explained why the baron was so harsh with me. I kind of knew already, as much as a child can." He tugged at a lock of hair. "No one on either side of my family is a ginger. I stuck out among my darker brothers. Anyway, my mother had done her best to shield me from his cruelty. I think she did so out of pride more than actual love for me. Maxwell did, as well, because he was her servant, not the baron's. And once she was gone, I was left with only that old man as my protector. He's not very effective, as you can imagine—not for lack of trying, mind, but because he's a servant. He has no control over anyone." He ate the rest of his food and didn't object when Evan gave him more.

"Hmm. I don't expect he is good at shielding, except he did his best for you when I kidnapped you. He stuck by you at the risk of his own life."

"I suppose that was partly out of loyalty to my mother, but it's also true that his life would have been forfeit if he'd returned without me. The baron only suffered his presence because he acted as my nursemaid."

"I think you underestimate Maxwell's feelings for you. He was clearly upset about your leaving. Everyone was."

"Including you?" He didn't know why he asked such a silly question. The brigand had no reason to see him other than as a bag of coin or a burden.

Evan cocked his head and smiled in a way that did funny things to Rory's stomach. "I was incandescently so. Slipping on a rock in that stream and knocking yourself unconscious to drown is only one of the many ways your short journey might have ended badly. Fortunately for the both of us, you lay a trail that was easy to follow."

Surprisingly pleased with the man's confession and also annoyed at his frank assessment of Rory's shortcomings as a soldier, he frowned. "I've never been trained in warfare. I have no skills in anything, in fact. Useless." He hated sounding sorry for himself, but the words tumbled out whether he wanted them to or not.

"Don't say that about yourself." Evan's tone was sharp. "You have much to recommend you."

Rory smiled wanly. "Name one admirable quality that I possess."

Evan didn't hesitate or search for something to say. "You have courage. Running out of here on your own instead of waiting for what you assumed was your fate required fortitude."

Rory snorted. "Running from death? Even a dumb animal has such courage." He shook his head and popped the last of his food in his mouth. "All I know of the world is what I've read in books, and even then, I've had only my mother's limited library to choose from. The baron is not a big reader. Hunting, fucking and eating are his strengths."

"But were you not headed to the university when I…abducted you." His tone implied that he felt guilty about what he'd done.

Rory wasn't used to powerful men acknowledging any fault or mistake. Evan was different from any he'd ever known before. Not only was he compelling as no other man had been, but he also had a kindness to him. It had showed during his nursing of him as well as now. With the immediate fear of being killed gone, he was able to relax enough to appreciate it.

He put the piece of bark down and huddled more in the tunic. The night was chilly, bordering on cold, despite the time of year. "I *was* going to the university. That's true. I'd dared to ask a few times before, hoping to escape the man's brutal reach and find something productive to do. He'd always said no, but a few weeks ago, he surprised me by bringing it up himself. I don't think he meant it as a boon." He could still see the cold calculation and hatred in the man's eyes as he'd told him to pack and go.

"You think he meant to get you out from under his feet?"

"I think he intended for me to die, either on the journey or perhaps he had sent men ahead of me to solve the problem of my existence once I arrived in the city. It's easy enough to blame a footpad or something. At the castle, too many eyes and ears would have known if he'd had me dispatched to an early grave. I think all his punishments were meant to kill me in a more natural way. I surprised us both by being stronger than I look, so killing overtly was something he wouldn't risk. Not that anyone at the castle would mind or dare confront him over it, but he wouldn't want such a tale to make its way back to the duchess. She doesn't seem to care about what he does normally, but perhaps murdering a supposed child might make her take notice."

Evan stiffened and shot his gaze sideways for a moment. "If you're right, I played right into his hands."

"When you first waylaid my carriage, I feared you had been sent to kill me. I was glad that you didn't, but then I knew you'd do so anyway because the ransom wouldn't be paid."

Evan shot his hand out and clasped Rory's arm. The touch sent a shudder down his spine that had nothing to do with the chilly air. "I was *never* going to hurt you. I won't now, either. The money was important, but my men and I have a code. Killing is not part of it, and killing the innocent is anathema."

Rory swallowed hard around a lump in his throat. "I'm glad to hear it." He hadn't intended to let the tears that had threatened since his captivity overtake him. The sob broke past his lips before he could choke it back. The next thing he knew, he was in Evan's lap, the man running his hand in circles on his back.

"There now, don't cry."

"I've been so scared. I can't remember a time when I wasn't." He slumped into the man, clawing at his vest with one hand. "What am I going to do now?"

Evan hugged him tight and rocked gently. "Hush. You don't need to worry about that. I have you."

"You can't keep me forever."

"Who says I can't?"

Startled at the comment, Rory pulled free enough to look at him. His mouth was close to Evan's, and he could see the way the man's pupils dilated and his nostrils flared. There was a hardness, too, pushing against his bottom. He knew what it was and understood its meaning. He should have been afraid of this obvious sign that the man wanted him. Out here away from everyone in the camp, Evan could do what he liked, and no one would be there to challenge him. Rory wasn't sure he himself would try to, either. There was something compelling about the potential intimacy. No one other than his mother had ever cradled him like this. Maybe it would okay to trust Evan with more of him.

"Do you want me?"

"More than my next breath." That was the only warning he gave before claiming Rory's lips with his own.

Rory had always thought kissing was a sloppy thing to do. He'd been wrong. At least in as much as there was nothing repellent about the way the man slid their lips against each other, sucking lightly and nipping gently. And when he pressed his tongue inside, it was another soft claiming, a languid exploration of Rory's mouth. It was Rory who tried to intensify the kiss, clasping his arm around Evan's neck and practically crawling through the man's skin. They were both hard and breathing harshly. When Evan shifted to have him straddle his lap, Rory understood that it would take nothing at all for the man to free himself and thrust his cock inside Rory's exposed ass.

Rory broke the kiss and gasped for air. "Do it," he whispered. "Take me. I want you to. I...*need* you to." The words tumbled out of him, crazy to his own ears, yet with his emotions running high with the knowledge that he wasn't going to be killed, he had a sudden and overwhelming urge to taste life the way it was meant to be.

Evan squeezed the breath out of him for a moment. Without saying anything, he reclaimed Rory's lips, and as he kissed him, he rocked Rory against his body, cupping his ass for leverage. It was slow at first, then increased in speed, the friction rubbing his dick against the cloth of the tunic. Rory panted and gasped into Evan's mouth. His pleasure rose and exploded without warning. He arched into Evan's hold and screamed.

Chapter Six

For the first time in the many days that Evan had slept beside Rory, the boy was curled into him instead of edging as far away as possible. It felt surprisingly right, as if his arms had been waiting to hold just this person. The small, lithe body pressed against his, torturing him in the best possible way. The ease in which he'd brought the lad to climax had been the most gratifying sexual pleasure he'd ever known. And the obvious release of tension that must have been building in Rory his whole life had sent the boy into almost instant slumber. There'd been no chance to even broach the idea of reciprocation, and Evan found he didn't mind. His dick would simply have to wait, as it had since the first time he'd lain down next to his captive.

He's not that now. The very notion that he'd sunk so low as to kidnap anyone, let alone this defenseless, abused boy, made him ashamed. His goal of helping those in the most need of it wasn't an acceptable excuse. He had to make things right for Rory, although how, he couldn't imagine. Sending him back to the baron was out of the question. That man could not be trusted, and what kind of life was waiting for Rory anyway? He had no means of supporting himself, and as young as he was, the baron would always exercise a legal right to govern his actions. Getting Rory to the university might help gain him his freedom, but the education there was costly. Whatever the baron had planned for his reputed son in sending him away to that city, the man wouldn't be inclined to do so now. If nothing else, this kidnapping was a good excuse to keep him close and maybe quietly get rid of him with poison and claim it was from abuse by his captors.

Rory murmured then sighed in his sleep, relaxing still in Evan's embrace. His beautiful face was smooth, unmarred by worry or anger. He looked impossibly young, and no matter his being drawn to the boy, Evan felt a fierce need to protect him. "You're mine, now," he whispered and closed his eyes to get some sleep of his own. The problem of what to do with his new charge was one that would have to wait until morning.

* * * *

Good sleep eluded him, so Evan reluctantly disentangled himself from Rory's limp body and went to the stream to wash himself in the frigid water. The return trek to the camp wouldn't take long. Instead of foraging for breakfast, he decided to hustle Rory back to take part in whatever Susannah was cooking. What he could see of the sky was clear, and the warmth of the day was burning off the chill of the night quickly. Rory should be fine with wearing just Evan's tunic. He liked the idea that something of his covered the boy. When he checked on their boots, he found both pairs were reasonably dry from the fire, despite their submersion. He pulled on his and considered whether he should wake the boy or let him rise on his own time.

The question became moot in the next instance as Rory yawned and blinked his eyes open. Sitting up, he rubbed the sleep from them and jerked his head to search for Evan. He relaxed immediately at the sight of him and shot him a pretty smile. "I thought for a moment you'd left me."

Evan ignored the offense he automatically took at such an admission. There had been no insult intended by it, he was sure. Rory needed to feel safe and not worry that his every word and deed would court punishment. "I would never do such a thing. You can count on me, Rory."

The boy looked at the ground. "Trust in someone isn't something I'm used to." He peered up at him from under his lashes. "I'd like to learn to do so with you."

"A lifetime of rejection and brutality will be hard for you to put aside, I imagine. I won't use words to convince you that I'm not like the baron. My actions show the world what kind of man I am."

Rory's cheeks flushed pink. "What you did last night certainly told me a lot." He licked his lower lip. "I'm sorry I fell asleep before reciprocating. Do you want me to…?" He shook his head on a chuckle. "I don't even know what to offer. You're the first person to ever touch me in that way."

Evan had known that already. "It was not my intent to seduce you. Your situation is too fraught at the moment for you to make a free decision. And I don't need anything in return. I'm glad I was able to bring you some pleasure."

Rory heaved a big sigh. "It was amazing. I don't usually…pay attention to that part of me. Maxwell is always by my side and sleeps on a pallet in my room. I'd be embarrassed for him to know, so I usually do nothing. Oh, wow, I think I'm getting aroused again." He looked at Evan with wide, guileless eyes.

Evan wasn't surprised by the news. His own dick had never fully softened, and now it was rock hard once more. And because his imagination could picture all kinds of ways to handle both of their problems, he shut it down. Rory was still too emotionally raw and scared to truly consent. He stood abruptly. "As tempting as that knowledge is, we should go back to the camp. I'm sure you're hungry and the others will worry until we return."

"All right. Whatever you say." The boy stood, and even as big as the tunic was, his erection was easy to see.

"Take a moment to freshen yourself in the stream. I'll wait here." He turned his back to resist the temptation to watch.

A few minutes later, Rory joined him, his face freshly scrubbed and his cock no longer showing. "Do you think my boots are dry enough?"

"They seemed to be when I checked. If you find that not so, I can always carry you back." Happy to have something to do that didn't involve thinking of Rory's dick, Evan went to fetch them. Kneeling in front of Rory, he helped him put them on.

The way the boy held on to his shoulder as he lifted one foot then the other was not so much arousing as a comforting indication that the boy truly was starting to trust him. Evan smiled as he stood and on impulse, held out his hand. If he couldn't have the pleasure of carrying the boy, he might at least be able to hold his hand. To his delight, after a moment of hesitation, Rory took it. His cheeks were once again pink, which was adorable. The brat was actually a shy boy.

The walk back to camp was shorter than the journey away from it had been. Not knowing the forest, Rory had taken a more roundabout path. Evan knew the shortest way, and they arrived just as everyone else seemed to be finishing their morning meal. His band erupted in cheers once they were spotted arriving. Everyone not on look-out duty surrounded them and bombarded them with questions. Rory pressed against his side and remained silent. Evan enjoyed how the boy was looking to him for protection.

Maxwell pushed to the front and grabbed Rory by his shoulder. "What were you thinking, foolish boy? I would have gone with you if you'd told me of your plans."

Rory leaned closer against Evan's side. "There was no point in both of us courting death. I knew you'd be fine here."

Dropping his hand, Maxwell sniffed. "As if I could ever live with the knowledge that you were out there, lost and likely dead. I made a promise to your mother, and I intend to keep it for the rest of my days."

Rory shook his head. "Oh, Maxwell, she's gone. I release you from your duty to protect me. It's past time for me to do that for myself."

Evan released his grip on Rory's hand to sling his arm around his shoulders and hug him tightly instead. "That's actually my job now. He's fine, old man, and will stay that way. I'll make sure of it."

"You?" the servant sneered. "A brigand? What do you intend, to make him part of your band as you waylay travelers? It's only a matter of time before your venture, however noble, will end with your head being cleaved from your body. The baron has even more reason to roust you now that he can claim you killed his son."

Evan tightened his grip. "I will never hurt Rory, let alone kill him."

"And do you think that inconvenient truth will matter to the baron? He makes his own rules and reality. If he says his son was murdered, then that's what everyone will believe. Only the Duchess of Windham has the power to rein him in, and she's proven indifferent to his antics."

Evan knew all too well how the duchess had failed to keep the baron in check. He felt that abdication of her duties a bitter pill to swallow, but he had no choice. Robbing the rich had been the only solution to the problem that he could think of. Still, he knew there were pieces of information about Rory that he needed yet didn't have. Maxwell had to be the best source of answers to his questions.

"Manfred, please take charge of Rory. He's in need of his breakfast."

The brother stepped forward with a kindly smile. "Of course, Evan. Come, my boy. Susannah has made a tasty porridge, and there is plenty left for the two of you."

Rory shrank away. "I want to stay with you, Evan."

Those words made his chest swell, but it wasn't the right thing at the moment to keep the boy with him. He gave into the impulse to kiss the top of the boy's head, then gently pushed him toward the monk. "I need to talk to Maxwell. Go with Manfred, and I'll join you soon."

Rory gave him a dubious look. "If you say so." With dragging feet, he went with the monk.

Evan waited until they were out of earshot. "Come on. I have questions, and you will give me the truth—the whole of it."

"Very well." The servant seemed resigned.

"I am sticking with the two of you," Maurice declared, and his expression dared Evan to challenge him on it. Maxwell's cheeks colored much as Rory's had, but he held his tongue.

Evan eyed both men. "As you like." He led them to a ring of rocks at the far side of the camp. It was a convenient place to sit and talk in a small group. Once they were all settled on their asses, Evan got right to the heart of what he wanted. "Tell me about Rory's father—the one who conceived him, not the baron, obviously."

Maxwell stared at his hands folded primly on his knees. "It's hard to speak of that, which I've sworn to keep secret. But," he added before Evan could interject, "I understand that matters have changed. It's past time for the truth to be told to someone. Not even Rory knows the details."

"I thought as much. Continue, and I will decide what of your tale I'll share with Rory."

The old servant offered a smile. "It's a relief to see that the boy has someone who will care for him other than me. I have no power, so I was of little help to him, other than to take his lickings when I could and help him recover when I couldn't.

"So, where to begin? The baroness, I suppose, is the genesis of Rory's predicament. I came with her when she married the baron, my family having served hers for generations. She was a beautiful woman, yet selfish and self-absorbed. In that way, she was a good match for the baron. I believe they hated each other on sight, but they did their duty, and once the baroness had produced an heir and a spare, they lived mostly separate lives."

"Well, that explains how the baron knew for sure that Rory wasn't his," Evan interjected.

"Indeed. His red hair notwithstanding, Rory couldn't possibly have been fathered by the baron. He hadn't visited the baroness' bed in a very long time." He frowned. "The baroness was actually faithful in her way. She didn't want him, but she didn't take lovers, either—not until that one fortnight one summer when another lord from the Outer Vale visited for some transaction involving the exchange of goods. Among his retinue was a young knight destined to serve in the king's guards. He was traveling with the lord for whatever reason, probably at his family's behest. I knew the moment the baroness set eyes on him that she wanted to take that boy to her bed...and she did."

"You're saying Rory's father is some randy knight who thought nothing of bedding a married woman?"

"Not exactly, sir. Yes, the knight fathered Rory, but the baroness gave him no choice. She used her position to pressure him into lying with her. I could see the boy didn't want to yet dared not refuse. And I can't blame him. When I tried to dissuade her from that folly, I got a flask thrown at my head. She was not a kind woman and used to getting her way with everyone except the baron."

"What was the knight's name?"

"I can't recall. My lady referred to him simply as 'boy', as if he'd been put there for her pleasure and was nothing more than—if you'll excuse the vulgarity—a cock attached to a handsome face."

"I see. It's a wonder the baron didn't turn her out when she came up pregnant," Maurice observed.

Maxwell treated the man to a warm smile. "Oh, he would never have done so. It would be tantamount to admitting he hadn't controlled what went on in his own castle. No," he added with a shake of his head. "Instead, he acted as if Rory were his son, while visiting petty cruelties on the poor lad. To her credit, the baroness shielded him from the worst of it. When she realized she was dying, she made me swear to take her place in that."

Agitated by the story, Evan couldn't sit any longer. He stood and paced around the ring. "You're a servant. What did she think you'd be able to do?"

"The baroness excelled at ignoring those facts that she didn't like. I've done my best…"

"But the baron has tortured Rory for all the long years since her death. No wonder he lashes out. He must be terrified at what horror will greet him at every turn."

"Just so, sir. Just so." Maxwell was quiet for a while, although he shot looks at Maurice, and the man smiled encouragingly in return. "What are you doing to do with the boy now that you know there will be no ransom?"

Evan threw up his hands and sat heavily back on the rock. "An excellent question. I have no idea."

"I suppose we must become members of your band."

"No." Evan shook his head. "That won't do. I can't picture you making a life here, no matter the incentive," he added dryly with a glance at Maurice. "And this is no place for a delicate lad like Rory—however much I might wish otherwise," he added in a low voice. "I must figure out a way to deal with the baron that doesn't involve highway robbery anymore."

"Ha!" This from Maurice. "And what has changed since the last time you gave this a good think?"

"Rory," was Evan's simple reply.

Maxwell harrumphed. "I dare not hope that there is a solution. There was one occasion in which I thought the baron would be put in his place. An envoy of the king turned up unexpectedly for a visit."

Evan straightened. "I'd heard as much, but nothing came of it." It had been his best hope that his plea had been heard and someone had been sent to help the people who'd been kind enough to put their trust in him.

"No, the baron coopted him the very first night. Coin was passed over, from what I could tell. And life under the baron went on as usual."

"Do you remember the envoy's name?"

"Tost, I believe. A pompous man, I dare say."

"I know that name." Evan stood once more, his hands on his hips, racking his brain for the memory of the man. "Ah." He snapped his fingers. No matter the life he led as a brigand in the woods, he still kept his ear to the ground to keep track of the doings at the palace. The man had been banished to the marshlands after Prince Soren had defeated the Marsher chief. *His male bride's father.* Because the reminder of that little and really unimportant detail gave him a fleeting and bad idea that he nevertheless had to consider, he refocused on the issue at hand. "He must have reported back to the duchess and the king that nothing was amiss—and that was that."

They were all silent for a while as they digested the information. "There is only one thing for it," Evan finally decided. "We must try again to get those in power over the baron to stop his evil ways."

Maurice stood, putting a comforting hand on Maxwell's shoulders before confronting Evan. "You told me that you'd sent word to the duchess about him. Are you suggesting you try again? What makes you think it will do any good this time?"

Evan ran a hand through his hair, struggling to get the words out. This new plan forming in his head was going to be far riskier than his idea to kidnap someone for ransom. "There are two reasons why. One is that the previous duchess is dead. An accident took her well before her time." Thinking of it opened the old wound of grief that he'd tamped down for years. "Her daughter holds those lands now, and she's barely older than Rory."

"So you think she may be more sympathetic than her mother."

"No. Her mother was a good woman but naïve in many ways. I'm sure she expected Tost to be honorable in his assessment. But he's gone from the court, so he won't be sent again, and we can only hope that this time, someone more reliable will tend to the matter. And," he added with a grimace, "the other reason I believe we'll have better luck this time is that we have Rory." He stared across the camp. The boy was sitting with Manfred and Susannah, still eating. "His word on the baron's perfidy will be a compelling testimony."

"You mean to send him to court?" Maxwell demanded with an expression of alarm.

"No. I mean to *take* him to court."

* * * *

Rory huddled by the cooking fire, a little chilly still from his night on the ground. Evan's tunic and the warmth emanating from his large body had kept him comfortable through the night, but the journey back to the camp and now sitting under the heavy canopy above had made him cold again. Sammy had kindly shared trousers with him, so his legs were covered, and while the boy had also offered him a tunic, as well, Rory perversely wanted to keep wearing the brigand's.

What has happened to me? The last twenty-four hours had been a whirlwind of emotions—fear, determination, sadness then most surprisingly of all, hope. Revealing his deep secret at last to someone had lifted a burden that had weighed him down his whole life. Evan had been so kind and understanding. No one had been like that with him, not even his mother or Maxwell. They hadn't been cruel like the baron—at least Maxwell hadn't been—but that was a low measure of how he should have been treated. And he wasn't a child anymore, so he hadn't reacted with relieved tears. Well, mostly hadn't. Instead, an urgent need had welled up inside him, one that was only partially assuaged by Evan's kisses and over-the-clothing humping. He'd thought that physical desire had been beaten down by him for lack of opportunity. Now that it had been woken, he was struggling to keep it in check.

He glanced over to where the brigand, Maxwell and Maurice discussed him and pondered his fate. There was no doubt about the purpose of that little conflab. He should resent being talked *about* instead of *to*, but so long as Evan chose to keep him, he wouldn't quibble.

Living the life of a highwayman wasn't a scary prospect. It was still better than being tossed back to the baron, and if the life came with Evan cocooning him with his big body and giving him pleasure, it was a future he could embrace. Of course, the man would demand more from him than a few kisses and cuddling. His hole spasmed at the thought of what was to come. The idea of being mounted might have frightened him but for the yearning he felt for the man.

He straightened as the men stood from their perches and came his way. None of them looked happy. That was not a good sign, yet he kept his focus on Evan's face, and as the man arrived, he treated him to a reassuring smile. *Everything will be all right.* Maybe he shouldn't believe in this man so much. He knew very little about him. The important stuff, however, such as trustworthiness and protective instincts, had been on full display since he'd been kidnapped. If he hadn't been angry, defiant and scared, he would have seen those qualities from the start.

Evan plopped down beside him and slung an arm around his shoulders. "Did you get enough to eat?"

Rory looked down at his empty bowl. "Yes, thank you. Susannah is very kind."

The woman scoffed at that. "Feeding a hungry boy is the least I can do. There's still some left for you, Evan." So saying, she ladled porridge into a bowl and added in some berries and nuts. "I imagine you've worked up quite an appetite yourself."

Evan grinned. "I certainly have. Chasing after an errant boy and fishing him out of a frigid stream is hard work." He squeezed Rory's shoulder to show he was only jesting before freeing his hand to take up his spoon.

Rory couldn't resist pressing closer to him. "What have you all decided?" It seemed to him that tackling the question head on was best. Although Maxwell and Maurice had sat nearby, as well, he didn't look to them for answers. Evan was in charge. Everyone recognized that.

Evan swallowed his mouthful before answering. "You and I are going to court to beg the Duchess of Windham and the king, himself, if necessary, to do something about the baron's reign of terror."

Rory's stomach tightened at the news. "Why? They both know about him, don't they? There was an emissary a few years back who seemed quite friendly with the baron by the time he left. And nothing changed. Nothing at all," he added with bitterness. For a couple of days, he'd actually harbored some hope that things would get better. The disappointment when they didn't had been hard to take.

"I have reason to believe that particular man didn't do his duty and reported back to the duchess and the king that all was well. The mistake I made was making the complaint without following it through personally. I won't do that again. This time I will plead my case in person and demand something be done."

Rory gnawed at his lower lip. This plan seemed incredibly dangerous. The baron was a nobleman and therefore someone who had the king's ear in a way that Evan and everyone else in the band of brigands, himself included, didn't. Barging their way into court and making demands was a good way to end up in the dungeons—or worse. Not even being the baron's supposed son would shift that power. Nemo and Manfred had wandered over to join them. They each frowned at Evan's words. He wasn't the only one to worry about the plan, apparently.

Rory believed that at the moment he was the best person to challenge their leader. He wasn't a stupid man, but his intentions sounded a bit crazy. "Evan, what makes you think you can get to the duchess, let alone the king, to make your case? That's assuming you're not recognized as the highwayman who has robbed a lot of the people who might have ended up at the palace."

Evan nodded. "I may very well be arrested on the spot for my deeds, but the duchess and the king will still hear me out."

His certainty seemed delusional. "How can you be so sure?"

With a sigh, Evan put down his now-empty bowl and turned to take Rory by his shoulders. "Because, darling boy, I am Evander, Lord of Windham, the duchess' uncle and the king's distant brother-by-marriage."

Chapter Seven

The sudden silence around the camp told Rory that he wasn't the only one hearing this revelation for the first time. It wasn't all that surprising. Evan was clearly an educated man who had grown up with some privilege. The fact that he was of the nobility was the part that was hard to swallow, let alone that he was part of the royal family.

He asked the obvious question. "How in the name of the gods did you end up a brigand?"

"It's a long story."

Rory frowned. "I think I speak for everyone one when I say we have time to hear it out." There were general murmurs of agreement from the others.

"Well, then." Letting go of Rory, Evan stood and walked outside the inner circle by the fire to speak. "I do owe all of you an explanation about who I really am and how I came to be here. We all have pasts that we want to keep to ourselves. Unlike most of yours, I'm not running from a terrible past. Quite the contrary.

"I am the second born of the old duke. When our father died, my older sister took his place and her marriage to Prince Soren meant she needed to spend most of her days at court. She asked me to be her castellan, an honorable profession for the second born but," he heaved a sigh, "it was a role I was ill-suited for. I never paid much attention to farming or managing accounts. The thought of arbitrating squabbles among her people seemed grim, as well. I am not a patient man and more suited to outdoor pursuits than pouring over ledgers. So I regretfully bowed out, something that infuriated my sister. I was…indifferent to her demands. It was not well done of me, but I was young and selfish enough to do as I liked. I set off to see the world, have some adventures and make my own fortune. I didn't do as much with either of those goals as I would have liked."

"So what, is this life a form of entertainment for you?" This from Nemo, and their eyes spit fire. Many of the others echoed the sentiment.

"No." Evan shook his head. "I hope you all know me well enough by now to understand that I am driven to do all of this because I cannot bear seeing people suffer." He paced away, then returned. "I came back to this part of Moorcondia because I was homesick and I had coin in my pocket to live an independent life. It was the baron's land that I passed through first, and my gods, the beaten-down and starving faces of the villagers I saw was like a punch to my gut. My father would never have allowed people under his domain to suffer like that. And I couldn't believe that my sister would, either."

Not liking the scowls he still saw on some of the band's faces, Rory interrupted. "You went to your sister then to tell her?"

"No. The first thing I did was use the wealth I'd amassed to get as many villagers through the winter as possible. Then, I sent word to my sister. When nothing happened, I believed that she was either so mad at me that she ignored my entreaties, or she'd been perhaps coopted by the royal family that was not as selfless as I'd thought and felt no concern for the people who labored in her duchy. And when she died suddenly and the duchy went to her oldest daughter, I assumed she would be the same.

"Knowing as I do now that Minister Tost was sent to check out the baron, I did her a great disservice. I failed everyone, actually. I should have gone to the capital and confronted her. But I've never been one to follow the rules, so instead, I decided to rob the rich and give the coin back to those who'd toiled for it." He shook his head. "I've been an idiot—an arrogant one."

Rory jumped to his feet and raced to hug the man around his waist. "No, you haven't been." He pressed his face against Evan's chest. "You made the right decision with the information you had. Because you stayed here, you've saved countless lives, I'm sure. If you'd gone to the palace and failed in your plea, nothing would have changed, and people would have been worse off because you might not have been able to come back here and do what you have been."

Evan wrapped his arms around him and kissed the top of his head. "My dear, Rory, I am amazed at how decent you've remained in the face of such vicious cruelty. I promise I will keep you safe, and I will do better for everyone else, too. The risk of confronting my niece and the king is worth it now, especially as I'm asking you to go with me to lend credence to my complaint. If you will. I won't force you to."

"Of course, I'll go." For the first time in his life, Rory felt as if he had purpose and a measure of power to make a difference, not only for himself, but for others, as well.

"Thank you." He punctuated his words with another kiss to Rory's head.

"You can't take the boy, Evan." Brother Manfred stepped forward. "Your tale doesn't surprise me. It was always obvious that you were noble born. And while I applaud your plan to go to the palace, taking Rory with you puts him at risk. If your plea goes unheeded, or even if it is, the baron still has legal rights over the boy. He can demand that he be returned to him, regardless of whether he's punished for what he's done."

Rory's breath caught at the thought of being back in that horrible man's control. He'd rather die than return to his old life or be dispatched at the man's hands. But these people and thousands of others needed his help. If this was the one thing he did in his life of value, it would be worth it. He pushed away to look up at Evan. "I'm willing to take the risk."

Evan smiled at him and softly ran his thumb across Rory's lips. "I'm not, which is why I'm going to marry you before we leave. As your husband, my rights over you will trump the baron's. Even if something happens to me, you will have a legal claim against the Windham estate for your upkeep. My niece will have no choice but to see to your care."

Rory froze and had trouble hearing Evan's words because of the buzzing in his ears. "M-marry?" He choked out the one-word question.

"Yes," Evan replied is a soft voice.

"But we're both men. Is that allowed?"

"It would seem so, as my brother-by-marriage, Prince Soren has broken whatever barrier there might have been on such a union. And Prince Ronan has done the same with the jarl from the Dark Mountains. We've all heard that news. If those men can have a male bride, why can't I?" He looked away. "I'm sorry if the thought of it doesn't please you. I must admit that if I could think of another way, I would take it, because you've had no choice in your life. I'm proposing that you put yourself under another man's control. I'm doing it to protect you the only way I know how."

Rory smashed himself against the man. "I accept."

So what if the proposal wasn't really a question and was driven by something far less romantic than love. Being married to this man wasn't a dream come true. He'd never dared to yearn for anything. The mere thought of it, however, sent a tingle down his spine that pooled into his cock. He wanted Evan, and more, he felt safe with him. Love was something out of books. Marriages had been successfully made on more practical concerns. If being Evan's wife meant ridding himself of the baron's control, it was reason enough. It would be fun, too, to see the man brought down a peg or two and thwarted in his despicable intent toward the bastard that he'd been forced to claim as his own son.

Evan's chest rose and fell on a deep breath. "Very well. Brother Manfred can perform the ceremony right now, then we can plan on our trip to the capital. We should leave tomorrow."

"Oh." Rory's head spun at the idea for everything happening immediately. He supposed there was no need to wait. It wasn't as if they were going to have a formal wedding or anything.

"Absolutely not!" Susannah stood with her fists on her waist. "A wedding takes some effort, Evan. Your bride shouldn't stand by your side in your cast-off tunic and borrowed trousers. He needs fussing over."

"Thank you, but that's not..." His words dried up at the woman's fierce look.

"You are a baron's son, for all that he is a fucker, and you're going to be a lord's wife. Even though your fancy clothes are lost, you should still go to court looking the best we can do. And we'll need a feast. There's always one for a wedding."

"Susannah, there is no need to go to any trouble," Evan started before he too shut his mouth when she stared daggers at him.

"It won't be like what you'd get at court, but we can do better than oatcakes and dried venison." She turned to Nemo. "Get hunting. We'll have fresh meat tonight."

Shooting a wry look in Evan's direction, they nodded. "Yes, ma'am." Then they strode away.

Everyone started moving now. Susannah was clearly in control...in this matter, at least.

Evan shrugged. "I suppose she is right. You deserve as nice a wedding as we can manage." He surprised Rory by bending to capture his mouth and kiss him with the same passion he'd used when they'd been all alone. By the time Rory was permitted to take a breath, he'd begun to be disappointed that Evan's plan of an immediate wedding had been thwarted. *I want him to claim me* now.

Something of his thoughts must have showed through because Evan chuckled. "I know, darling. I can hardly wait to bed you." He frowned. "You do know that I must to bind our marriage. The baron could petition to annul it if I don't."

Rory felt his cheeks heat. "Of course, I know. And...I want you to." Taking the man's hand, he pressed it against the place where his dick strained the structural integrity of his borrowed trousers. "I know what being married means, Evan. Last night was the best time I've ever had. I expect it gets better from here on, yes?" He wasn't so sure. There would be at least some pain, he knew that much. Maybe the pleasure that the man could wring out of him would make up for that.

"Cheeky boy." Evan tapped Rory's nose. "Susannah is right, you know. You will have as good a wedding as any brigand's camp has ever held. Now, I'll leave you in her capable hands and start figuring out the safest and fastest route to the palace."

Rory watched his soon-to-be husband walk away, appreciating how nice he looked from that view. His muscular ass was easy to see, even with his long vest covering it. Rory could imagine how much power there was to drill his ass with when the time came. His hole clenched at the thought, and his dick throbbed. His cheeks felt hotter as Susannah approached him with a knowing look. His desire for Evan must have been easy to read in his expression.

"Come on, now. Let's see what we can do to make you the prettiest bride ever." She smiled and winked, making him laugh.

He let her take him away, trusting that she would know what to do.

* * * *

Evander was surprised at the nerves plaguing his stomach. The idea of marrying Rory had come on the fly, the logical thing to do if he was going to take the boy to court and expose him once more to his father's power. The truth be told, he would have convinced himself and everyone else of its necessity, regardless. Since their brief interlude by the stream, his desire for the boy had been unleashed. When he'd been a captive, there'd been no question of trying to seduce him. Now that the barrier was gone, and it was impossible for him to ignore how much he wanted to gather the boy in his arms and sink himself into what would be undoubtedly a tight and virginal ass. His cock had been so hard the entire day, it was a wonder he could walk.

Everyone had gone to a lot of trouble to make the occasion special. A bower had been constructed of branches and vines with flowers entwined in them to give it a lovely, special look. Nemo, with the help of Cath, had gone deep into the woods to bring down a wild boar. The scent of it roasting made him salivate, but it was nothing compared to the hunger he felt when he saw Rory walking shyly toward him. Susannah and the other women who made the camp a home had done a wonderful job of tailoring a new tunic and trousers that weren't as fine as the ones he'd come to them with but far nicer that the worn ones he'd borrowed from him and Sammy. Evan had loved seeing his bride wearing his too-big tunic. This was more practical, however. He'd look fine when they got to court, and the cut of the cloth showed off his lithe body. And his lovely red hair was braided down his back with flowers twined with it.

As he approached, Rory treated him to a shy smile. There was nervousness in his eyes, but that wasn't all. Desire showed through, as well, more proof that the boy wanted him. He wagered that Rory was looking forward to their wedding night, as he was. Despite the custom of a morning wedding, he thought it made more sense to do it in the evening. It meant spending the rest of the night in the embrace of one's new spouse. He tried to tug his trousers to make room for his straining dick. Maurice caught his eye and smirked.

He ignored the man and returned his focus to his bride. When Rory reached him, he took the boy's hand

and brought the back of it to his lips for a kiss. "You are the most beautiful creature in these woods, and I am the luckiest of men."

Rory stifled a giggle. "You've made your own luck, it seems, given that you brought me here."

Evan's stomach clenched. He would hate himself for kidnapping the boy, except he wouldn't have met him otherwise. "I shall use the rest of my life to make up for that appalling treatment."

"I'm not complaining. Your stealing me away from the baron is the best thing that's happened to me."

Brother Manfred joined them before Evan could formulate a reply. "Are you ready, my lords?"

Rory replied before Evan could. "Yes, but I'm not a lord."

"No matter, my dear," Evan replied with some pride. "You'll soon be a lady."

* * * *

The feast was magnificent, but Evan ate lightly. The night would prove strenuous, and he wanted to have the right level of vigor for his duty as a new husband. That was a hard thing to get used to, although not as much as being accustomed to referring to the pretty boy sitting next to him as 'wife'. The oddity of it all paled, however, in comparison to the fierce sense of possession he felt whenever he thought of it. *My wife.* He'd never expected to take on that role, having no interest in being tied down and not needing to produce an heir. Merida had done an admirable job of continuing the family line. Her death had been a mighty blow, but at least she'd lived the kind of family life she'd always wanted. There would still be no children for him, and that didn't bother him. Living the rest of his life with Rory would be satisfying enough. He hoped the boy felt the same way.

There was laughing, music and some mead being passed around. It was good to give his people a reason to be merry. They had little of that in their lives, survival and helping the weak and needy being what gave them purpose. He hated leaving them. Maurice could be trusted to move them to a new camp for extra caution. Still, he had a troublesome feeling deep in his gut that he might not ever seen any of them again. No matter how the duchess and the king chose to deal with the baron, it didn't change the fact that he had repeatedly committed highway robbery. The king couldn't simply ignore that transgression, no matter the reason behind it. As long as Rory was cared for, he wasn't going to worry about his fate.

And there was no reason to dwell on those troubling thoughts this night, not when he had an enticing new bride to take to bed. Well, his pallet. There too, Susannah had done something special. A cozy and soft haven had been created at the far corner of the camp. It wouldn't provide much privacy, but it would have to do. Hopefully he'd have at least one chance to bed his wife in the luxury he deserved.

Unable to wait any longer, Evan leaned over to whisper into Rory's ear. "Shall we make our goodnights, darling?" The endearment tripped of his tongue naturally. He hoped Rory appreciated it.

His wife smiled at him. "Whatever you say."

Evan's heartbeat tripped. "Don't give me such power, wife. You have no idea how ravenous I can be."

"Show me."

That was all the encouragement he needed. Springing to his feet, he pulled Rory up with him. "On behalf of my wife and myself, I thank you all for your generosity and kindness. And I bid you good night."

There was a round of ribald comments and even some clapping. Those who played the lute and the recorder serenaded them to their resting place. A curtain had been strung up on a limb as a small measure of privacy. Ushering Rory past it, Evan let it drop, closing them in. The sound of the music faded as they were left on their own. When he judged them well away, Evan gave into the passion that had been building since the morning. He took his wife into his arms and claimed his luscious mouth.

Rory melted into him, a show of such complete trust that it humbled Evan. This boy, who had every reason to shy away from a large man, instead offered himself up for whatever Evan intended to do. It was hard to temper his own needs, to keep from tumbling the boy onto the soft pallet below, strip him and show him the passion boiling within. If Rory had been experienced, Evan would have done just that—for the first time. Take the edge off both of them with a fast, hard fuck, then use the rest of the night to worship him as he deserved. But Rory was an innocent of what transpired between two men. Oh, he undoubtedly knew the basics, might even have witnessed it in its uglier forms. What would pass between them this night, though, would set the boy's view of what his life would be like, and Evan would rather twist his own dick into a knot than put any fear or disgust in his wife's eyes.

Breaking off the kiss with a low moan, Evan cupped Rory's face with both hands to stare into his eyes. In the waning light, he could still see them clearly enough to know that while there was some uncertainty, there was no fear. It was important to set expectations of what was to come before the descension of night left only shadows visible. The idea of using his hands to explore his wife in the dark piqued his desire, but at the moment, words were needed.

"I don't want you to be afraid of me."

"I'm not. I've never been, because my whole life I've lived with bad men. I know them when I see them. You never had their look…even when you made me mad enough to scream," he added with a quick smile.

Evan's heart swelled at that reassurance. It humbled him that the boy could see his true self, even under such trying circumstances. "You can't know what your words mean to me."

"I'm glad they please you and…you don't have to woo me, Evan. I'm your wife now and understand my duty."

Those words had the opposite effect on his mood. Evan squeezed Rory's face briefly before saying, "I want you to enjoy this first time, as much as any virgin can. You are not simply my toy to take out and play with whenever the mood strikes me. We are in this marriage together, and this humble bed of ours is intended to be a place of pleasure for both of us."

"I have no doubt you'll be careful with me. And, you should know that I want this as much as you do." The boy leaned into him, allowing their bodies to press against one another. The hardness of his arousal brushed Evan's thigh.

He couldn't help grinning at the obvious sign and doubled down his determination to make this night good for his wife. "Let me take care of you, precious boy."

He brought his wife's face closer to his own to deliver another kiss. This time he took extra care to caress the soft lips and explore the warm mouth with languid strokes of his tongue. With a soft sigh, Rory melted into his embrace, then mewed his displeasure when Evan broke the kiss.

"Don't worry, darling. I'm only getting started."

Chapter Eight

Rory let his husband play with him as if he were a doll, stripping him of his clothing, then laying him down on the soft pallet. With the light nearly gone, he could see little more of the man than a shadowy shape moving him this way and that. It was better probably for this first time to be done in the dark. As much as he liked looking at Evan, he wanted his own nervousness to be hidden. Evan was too good a man to ignore any sign of distress, and while part of him wanted to put off what was to come because of ignorance and fear, more of him was keen to experience what he hoped would be a glorious explosion of pleasure. The bit of experience he'd had by the stream led him to believe that sex between two people was sufficiently wonderful to explain all the stupid things he'd seen and read about what other people did in pursuit of it.

I'm ready for this.

He lay docilely on the pallet just as Evan had arrange him and caught glimpses of the man as he shed his own clothing. When he knelt beside him, Rory got his first look at his husband's cock. Long and thick, it didn't disappoint, although it did beg the question of how he was supposed to accept such a thing inside his comparatively small body. He dared to reach out to touch it, snatching his hand back when the dick seemed to jump in response.

Evan chuckled softly and grabbed Rory's hand to bring it back to the shaft. "Touch me however you want, darling. I certainly intend to lavish my attention on every bit of you." He wrapped his own hand around Rory's and forced it to clasp the hardness Evan so proudly displayed. "See how much it likes you?"

"Hmm." It felt almost independently alive, not merely a part of the man. The skin was both silky smooth and bumpy where veins bulged out from it. It was far warmer than his fingers, and he could detect a pulsing, like a heartbeat. He dared to swipe his thumb across the head. A sticky substance coated it, and the movement made his husband groan. "Will it fit?" The question popped out before he could stop it.

Evan chuckled again and leaned over to kiss him sweetly. "It will, and I'll be careful," he whispered against his lips. Then he unclasped both their hands and put Rory's back to his side. "And you'll need to be careful as well not to send me over the edge too soon. Your very look could make me climax, and the touch of your fingers is a potent force for me to resist. I want to come inside you," he added before licking the outside of Rory's ear. "Let me play with you first."

Shuddering from the simple touch, Rory could only nod. His body was alive, every part of him sensitive and every touch sending waves of pleasure right down to his own cock. He was hard, with aching balls and a hammering heart. He didn't expect he would last long himself with the way Evan was playing with him. He'd known about kissing, of course, as a prelude to sex. But the way his husband lavished attention on his jaw, neck and shoulders was a revelation to him. Such mundane areas shouldn't produce pleasure, yet they did. Rory started panting, his breath laboring more with each new touch. And when his husband first licked, then sucked on a nipple, Rory jerked up and nearly squeaked.

Evan merely laughed and proceeded to do the same with the other one. This was a new surprise. Men were always grabbing women's breasts, and he'd seen how they liked to suck on them a time or two. The baron had encouraged public ribaldry in his hall. It had never occurred to Rory that a man would want to taste another man in this way—or that there was pleasure to be had by the one being sucked. He curled his fingers against the pallet, trying to be quiet and still. His cock had other ideas. With a jerk, it erupted all on its own. His breath caught in his throat, and he went ridged with the ecstasy of it. Only his well-honed ability to hide his reactions from others kept him from screaming into the night.

For a few seconds after his mind cleared, he feared his husband would be angry at his lack of control. Instead, Evan surprised him by barely pausing in his attention, working his way down Rory's chest, stomach and abdomen to end up lapping the skin where Rory's seed had spilled. He almost tried to stop the man, thinking it must be unpleasant to taste and swallow another man's cum. Then he relaxed with a reminder to himself that Evan knew what he liked. If he was doing exactly what he wanted, Rory may as well continue to lie back and enjoy it.

Because his husband lavished attention all around Rory's dick, including licking his balls and the sensitive parts of his inner thigh, it didn't take long before he was hard once more. When Evan ran his tongue up the hard shaft, Rory quivered with a surge of pleasure that threatened to make him come again. He wondered how many times it was possible to find such pleasure in a single night. Unfortunately, he wasn't going to find out any time soon.

With a *tsk*, Evan clamped his fist around the base of Rory's cock. "Not yet, darling. Keeping you aroused will help me gain entry."

Rory instinctively stiffened and squeezed his hole before forcing himself to relax again. He had to trust his husband. The man jerked his cock slowly while using his knee to force Rory's legs apart. He positioned his large body between them, spreading him wide. Then he fussed with something nearby before slipping his free hand between Rory's butt cheeks.

"Bend your legs, darling."

Rory didn't hesitate to comply and was rewarded by a fingertip making lazy circles around his puckered hole. The touch was so light and gentle that he had no trouble letting go of the instinctive tension of having someone play with the sensitive entry to his body. When Evan slid that finger inside, it was easy to take. There was none of the expected pain. Indeed, he shuddered with delight when it scraped against his prostate. Anatomy books made it seem so inconsequential, but he now knew that wasn't nearly the case. It was as if that one little spot lit up all his nerves. As Evan brushed over it again and again, Rory quivered uncontrollably and would have come another time but for his husband's choking it off with his fist.

Rory wanted to beg his husband for release. Once more, he called upon a lifetime of learning to acquiesce to the more powerful, although now he did so because he knew he was in good hands, not bad. Everything Evan did was no doubt in furtherance of bringing them both pleasure. As the second finger joined the first, he focused on all the good feelings and not about how much his hole was going to be tested. The rhythm of the gentle thrusting made him more languid. He focused his attention on the feel of the in and out, stretching his channel in such an organic and slow way that he stopped worrying about the possibility of pain.

Evan pulled his two fingers out, leaving Rory perversely bereft. His hole felt needy with its emptiness. The situation changed again as Evan returned to insert three slick fingers. This stretch was harder to take. Rory tensed again and fought to regain his sense of relaxation and pleasure.

"Easy," Evan soothed. "Breath steady now, in and out. That's it, darling. You are so beautiful. I can't wait to be inside you."

His husband's sweet words made Rory smile. Soon, the pleasure once more overrode the mild discomfort, and he drifted in a state of being on the edge of climax. Evan brought him to completion with a suddenness that left him once again in a shuddering pool of bonelessness. Before he understood what was happening, his legs were being held up by Evan's hands clutching the backs of his thighs and the blunt head of the man's cock pressed against his spasming hole. It was past the puckered barrier before Rory could fully register what was happening. Now the pain was biting, and he felt as if he were being stretched to the point of splitting wide open.

Letting go with one hand, Evan loomed over him and took his lips in a fierce kiss that derailed Rory's thinking and refocused him on the tongue invading his mouth. Evan pushed his cock in farther, leveraging Rory's leg that he still held and angling his body in a way that pressed his shaft against Rory's sensitive spot. It made him quiver as the sparks of pleasure warred with the discomfort of being filled. He panted into his husband's mouth and moaned as yet another climax built. He surprised himself by wrapping his leg around Evan's muscular ass in a silent command to do more. His husband didn't disappoint. He thrust deep and hard. His dick swelled inside Rory's ass before releasing a flood of warm cum. His own seed splashed once more against his stomach. And in that moment, he understood what he'd been missing in life – something that he now craved to have for the rest of it.

* * * *

"I could have ridden on my own, you know."

Evan smiled at the back of his wife's head, imagining the frown on the boy's face. "The farrier only had four to spare, and it makes far more sense for us to share than Brother Manfred, Nemo or Maxwell, I'm sure you'll agree. Besides, the feel of your rump against my lap is a delightful way to spend the tedious journey."

"Huh!" Rory sounded aggrieved, yet the brat wiggled his ass closer. "You'll have to wait until we make camp to soothe your need."

The prim, teasing tone his wife used nearly made him come right then and there. He briefly contemplated letting the others overtake them so that he could see how well he could manage fucking while astride a horse. He dismissed the thought, of course. No doubt his newly deflowered wife needed time to recover…and the horse probably wouldn't like it either. He found himself grinning like a fool, despite the seriousness of their journey.

"I wish we could go faster." The plaintive observation tugged at his heart.

"Once we are free of the baron's lands, we can use the road. It will still take some days to reach the palace, but at least the ride will be easier."

It wasn't quick to travel by horseback at a walking pace through the forest, but he dared not yet use the open and direct way to give them the full advantage of riding. The chances of being seen and stopped were too great. The baron's men would recognize Rory, if nothing else, then take them or kill them before the trip had barely started. That risk wasn't worth it. Once they'd cleared the baron's lands, anyone they came across would have no particular reason to scrutinize them. He'd donned his signet ring for the first time in years, as well, in case they were stopped by soldiers for any reason. That sign of his noble house, along with the disarming presence of a monk and an old servant, should keep them out of trouble for the trip. Rory was also obviously well-born and although young, not a child, only a young man traveling with his new husband. Nemo was the one unusual member of their group, but they had a way of blending into the shadows so that no one noticed them.

"Do you think the others are all right? I worry that the baron will send soldiers into the woods near where you took me and discover them."

Evan was heartened to hear his wife's worry about his people. So much had changed in such a short period of time. The boy probably hadn't truly processed what had happened to him, and Evan feared there would a moment soon when he might have a meltdown. In the meantime, it wasn't difficult to ease his mind.

"We are used to breaking camp quickly and always have the next site already picked before we settle down anywhere. Maurice can be trusted to get everyone to the new location without trouble. The man was raised in a castle among a noble family, the same as you and I. He knows what to do, and when this wretched business with the baron is over, he'll guide the others back to living honest lives with no one the wiser as to their brigand ways."

"Will we see them again, do you think?"

A tricky question. Evan was fairly certain he wouldn't, but he didn't want to worry his wife about his future. Dealing with the baron was what mattered, and if they succeeded in that, Evan wasn't going to care about his own fate—except the idea of being separated for the rest of his life from this darling boy he now called 'wife' was like a bitter pill in his mouth. "I'm certain of it, if that's what you want." *Some truth with only a bit of a lie wrapped in.*

Rory relaxed against him, his head fitting neatly under Evan's chin. "I'm glad. I don't know them very well, but they were kind to me. I wish Maxwell had stayed with them," he added in a lower voice. "I'm sure he and Maurice have developed some feelings for each other, and he'd be happier with him."

"He is a loyal man, and he won't leave your side until he's sure you have secured a good life for yourself."

Rory sighed. "That already happened the moment I married you. I'm Lady Evander Windham now, am I not?"

Having never cared one way or another about his title, Evan nevertheless puffed with pride at the sound of his wife's new title. "Yes, you are."

"It's weird to be known as a woman, but it's wonderful to think of myself as that and not the Honorable Rory Finley. It's never been mine to claim rightfully anyway. After we've done what we must, I don't want to ever hear that name again. It's funny, isn't it? I've been insisting that I'm not a lord and that's true. But now I'm actually a lady. Life has taken a funny turn—a delightful one, though," he assured Evan over his shoulder.

Evan smiled and kissed the top of his wife's head. "You shall only hear me call you 'darling' from now on, if it pleases you. I will reserve the use of 'Rory' or 'my lady' for when I'm mad."

Rory giggled as he'd hoped he would, and gathering him as close as possible, they continued on their way.

* * * *

Evan had stopped at the edge of the woods surrounding the capital to give Rory and the others a chance to see the palace where they were headed. It was a magnificent sight, and he expected that his niece would provide them with decent quarters within it, or at the very least, find them accommodations in the city fit for a nobleman, his wife and their entourage. He wanted to give Rory that comfort after spending long days living rough. Even after they'd cleared the baron's domain, there hadn't been enough coin to spend on inns. He'd left the band with as much money as possible, because they would need it, no matter the outcome of this trip. As a lord of Windham, he could ask his niece for a stipend, which would benefit Rory, if not himself. Although he didn't speak of it to any of the others, he strongly suspected that he wasn't going to enjoy the nicer parts of the king's home for very long.

Rory placed his palm against his stomach. "I'm nervous now that we've arrived." He turned to look at Evan. "What if they throw us in the dungeon?"

With a grin that hid his own concerns, he pressed a chaste kiss to those lovely lips. "My family will welcome you with open arms, darling. Have no fear of that." He'd been careful with his words because he wanted to speak only the truth at this point.

He signaled the others to continue and led the way past the city gates and up the long road to the palace steps. The guards didn't pay them any attention, which was not surprising, given that hundreds of people passed through here every day—merchants and travelers of all sorts. The real test would occur once they reached the bailey. In the meantime, he led his party slowly through the city, giving Rory in particular time to take in the sights. He doubted the boy had ever seen more than the castle he'd grown up in and the surrounding villages.

The soldiers guarding the bailey gates became alert at their approach but not overtly menacing. As he'd predicted, he and his entourage didn't appear threatening.

"Stay here," he ordered before handing the reins to Rory and getting off his horse. He took a moment to smile reassuringly at his wife, who sat with a straight back and a look of calm across his pretty face.

He went to stand between Nemo and Manfred astride their horses. "You've served us well, my friends and seen us safely to this point. Please feel free to take your leave of us and enjoy what the capital city has to offer." He lowered his voice to keep Rory from hearing his next words. "There is no need to take this risk. The responsibility is mine alone."

Nemo looked at Manfred. "Do you hear something? It's like the buzzing of a fly, annoying and meaningless."

The monk shrugged. "Give it up, Evan. We go where you do."

He was not surprised by their response, and knowing they both could see to themselves well enough, he put their potential sacrifice out of his mind. As he approached the guards, Evan removed his ring. He held it up for inspection when he was close enough to one of the men. "I am Evander, Lord Windham, and have come to visit my niece, Princess Eleanora, Duchess of Windham." He gave a haughty look that he'd learned while he was still in leading strings.

The guard narrowed his gaze as he scrutinized the signet, then stepping back, he nodded. "You may proceed through the gates, my lord. But please wait while we send a runner to the castle to see if her highness will receive you."

"Make it quick," he snapped. It was surprisingly easy to slip back into old habits. Those who ruled didn't need to worry about being polite to others, although his parents had taught him that kindness cost nothing. If it weren't so urgent that he get Rory to a safe place, he might have tried that now. He didn't think these hard-bitten soldiers would respond to it as well as brusque orders.

The others clustered their horses around his as they waited to be allowed up to the palace steps. Nemo swiveled their head around in unabashed curiosity. "So, this is how you lived before taking up highway robbery."

Evan tamped down a spark of annoyance. By keeping his band in ignorance of his connection to the king, he'd done them all a disservice. They were entitled to voice their displeasure however they pleased. "No, this is how the royal family lives. Windham Castle is not quite so grand, but I've visited here on occasion," he added with a quick grin.

"Let's hope they remember that and welcome us with open arms."

They didn't have long to wait. A page rushed out and down the steps. Grooms came out of the shadows to take their horses. As they walked up to the large double doors, Rory clutched his hand. Evan drew him in close and gave a squeeze of comfort. Just inside, a woman whom he could only assume was one of Eleanora's ladies in waiting stood to greet them.

She executed a deep curtsy. "Welcome, Lord Windham. Her grace is delighted to receive you." Her gaze swept over the others, pausing to scrutinize Rory, then giving a shallow curtsy to Manfred. "Welcome, brother." The others she dismissed with a flick of her head. "Her grace is having a room readied for you in the family wing."

"Excellent. I'm sure my wife and I will find the accommodations acceptable." He hugged Rory by the waist in case his meaning wasn't clear.

No doubt accustomed to Prince Soren's unusual marriage, the woman barely batted an eye. "Welcome, my lady." She was wise enough to show Rory the proper courtesy. "If you will follow me. Your servants will be shown to their quarters." She gestured to a page to tend to that. "Will you be staying with the monastery in the city, brother?"

"Not if I can help it," Manfred replied with great cheer. "I'm sure wherever my companions lay their heads will do very well for me, too."

The lady nodded in agreement before turning gracefully on her slippered feet. "This way, if you please, my lord, my lady."

Evan had to tug a little to get Rory moving. "Everything will be fine. I haven't seen my niece in many years, but she has always been a kind person. My ill thoughts of her earlier were not well done of me." He believed his own words. Nora wouldn't hold anything against Rory and would take care of him now that he was a member of the family. He just wasn't so sure of his own welcome.

He could have found the way, of course, but protocol was required, so he followed the woman up the stairs and down the corridor that led to the wing of the palace occupied by Soren and his family. As they went, the denizens of the palace scrutinized them with open curiosity. Their lives were exceedingly dull as far as he was concerned. The excitement caused by the arrival of a wayward lord and an unfamiliar nobleman was a nice break in their day. No doubt, people nearby had heard him introduce Rory and word of who he was had spread ahead of them. Court gossip was like wildfire.

Evan nodded to those he recognized, keeping a smile on his face as if he'd been gone only a few months and not the years that it had been. His nieces had been quite young the last time, the youngest not even born.

He felt shame over how little attention he'd paid his dear sister Merida and her family. Now it was too late to see her again. He hoped he'd have a chance to at least rectify the estrangement with his nieces.

The lady stopped at a door and knocking once, opened it. Then she stepped aside and ushered them in with a sweep of her arm before shutting the door behind them. The sitting room was empty other than a single woman standing by the window. For a moment, Evan's heart stopped. She looked that much like her mother—tall with her back straight and covered in a gown of simple elegance. When she turned, however, other than the frown of disapproval on her face, Nora was clearly her own woman.

She fisted her hands on her waist. "Well, uncle, so good of you to pay us a visit after all these years. I suspect you want something from me, given that you didn't manage to make it to your own sister's funeral."

Evan took the chastisement in his stride, because she was not wrong. But there was time enough to get down to business. At the moment, he wanted to calm Rory's nerves and present him in a more formal way.

He bowed. "Your grace, there is much for us to discuss, that's true. For now, I am pleased to introduce to you my wife, Rory." He let go of the boy so that he too could make a proper greeting.

With a courage that made Evan swell with pride, Rory stepped forward. "I am pleased to make your acquaintance, your grace. And thank you for welcoming us into your home." As pretty and as steady as his words were, the boy still reached behind him for Evan's hand.

He took it and drew the boy back to his side. "I apologize for the unannounced visit, but as you remarked, we have a lot to talk about. And yes, I do need your help," he added with a grimace.

Nora narrowed her gaze. "I'm sure you do, but before we get to the reason for your arrival, I demand to first know...how have you enjoyed being a brigand?"

Chapter Nine

Rory tried not to show how nervous he was as he and Evan bizarrely sat having tea with the princess, who was also their liege lady. After dropping the verbal equivalent of an anvil on their heads by revealing that she'd known what her uncle was up to all along, Nora, as she'd said he should call her, had rung for servants to fetch them refreshments. The same lady who had showed them up to the duchess in the first place oversaw the provision of a steaming porcelain pot of tea and various foods of small sandwiches and dainty sweets. She handed Rory his cup, doctored as he'd requested, as if he were her most honored guest. It was a strange turn of events, given that he'd expected soldiers to burst through any moment and drag them away.

"Thank you, Clarissa," the duchess said before sipping at her own cup.

The woman took it as the dismissal it was and herded the servants out, closing the door firmly behind them and herself. Evan handed Rory a sandwich of some kind of fish paste and smiled reassuringly at him. He nibbled and drank and switched his gaze between his husband and the duchess until he thought he might scream from the silence.

The duchess put down her tea. "So, let us begin with more pleasant topics." She looked at Rory. "Your wife, you say?"

"Yes," Evan replied cheerfully over the rim of his cup. "I'm sure he'll get along famously with your stepmother." He frowned. "Stepfather?"

"We call him Father Taryn, my sisters and I. No one pretends that he is a woman, if that's your question. And yes, I suspect he'll be a good companion to your Rory and guide him in what it means to be in his unusual situation. In fact," she added, selecting a pink frosted mini-cake, "his former dresser, now Lady Tentrees, is also visiting. Father Taryn insisted that he and his husband be quartered in our wing. That means I have nothing other than a single room to offer you and your wife. Better than sleeping on the ground, I imagine." With a quick, biting grin, she sank her teeth into half of the cake.

"Hmm." Evan put down his teacup and lounged back in his chair as if he were the lord of the manner. "My marriage is entwined with my purpose for coming here and how I've lived my life for these last few years."

"I'm keen to hear the details. We missed you at my mother's funeral." Her expression and tone showed hurt. "It was so very hard for all of us. We would have welcomed your presence, as there was no one from the Windham side of our family."

Knowing that her words must be cutting his husband to the quick, Rory reached for his hand and clasped it. He kept his gaze steady on the duchess. "You must hear Evander out. Everything he's done has been in service to others."

"My dear." Evan pulled their hands up to kiss the back of Rory's. "As usual, your courage brings me to my knees with gratitude." He switched his focus to his niece. "I will tell you first that Rory is blameless for any of my deeds. I stole him away for ransom, thinking Baron Finley would pay dearly for his son." He heaved a breath. "I was wrong. And I will tell you everything, but Rory has had a long journey and he need not hear this sad tale again. His life has not been easy, I will tell you that much. I want him to have the care and safety that my name and position can bring."

The princess' expression softened when she looked at Rory. "Of course. You are a Windham now and a member of the king's extended family. You are welcome, and I will see to your comfort and care." She reached behind her to pull a rope to ring for the servants. Her door opened immediately and once more the lady in waiting appeared. "Take Lady Windham to his chamber and inform the Duchess of Vostguard of his arrival."

Rory froze. He didn't want to leave Evan. It didn't matter if his story brought up painful memories. His duty was to stick by his husband's side. But Evan gave him no choice. Standing, the man tugged him to his feet, and with a soft kiss and a reassuring smile, sent him on his way.

Before the door shut behind him, he heard the princess' voice. "I will have answers, uncle. *Now*!"

Rory tried to turn around, but Lady Clarissa proved adept at keeping him moving forward without actually touching him. She led him down the corridor to the far end, then opened another door. It was a single bedchamber, although hardly simple. It was bigger and more luxurious than what he'd grown up in. The large canopy bed was dressed in dark blue silk. The furniture was made of a deep brown wood and upholstered with vivid silk patterns to match the bed covers. There was a fireplace at one end and lots of pretty candlesticks and other things that he wasn't sure he knew what they were for or that he'd ever need. He dared to wander around, his feet silent on the thick rug, touching all the smooth and soft materials. It would be amazing to live in this room for a few days, but he shouldn't get too comfortable. His life with Evan was uncertain, no matter the duchess' reassurances of her generosity. They could very well end up tossed out on their ears to live once more in the woods. He didn't mind the idea. Not really. As long as he was with his husband, any type of life was fine with him. *Why is that so? How can I be so certain?* Some part of his mind told him that it was love, but he turned away from the idea. That emotion made him too vulnerable. It was enough that he enjoyed being with the man. Eyeing the bed, he couldn't wait to find out how great it would feel to be mounted in such comfort.

"The Duchess of Vostguard, my lady."

Rory was just trying to work out what the woman was saying when a boy about his age swept into the room, dressed in a finery that defied his expectations of what a wife to a prince might wear. It was more feminine than typical men's attire, but his masculinity was also still obvious. Just behind him came another person, this one dressed in a lovely gown but also with a masculine look to his pretty face. And a third boy joined them, wearing the kind of tunic and trousers fit for a prince yet with the golden skin of someone who spent a great deal of time outside. Rory stood, his mouth agape, unable to think of a single thing to say.

The duchess solved that problem for him. "Rory, is it?" The boy grabbed both of his hands and smiled beautifully at him. "I'm so happy to meet you, and I know Nora and her sisters are excited to have their uncle visiting after so long."

His childhood lessons in decorum kicked in. He bowed as best he could while still in the enthusiastic grip of his distant brother-by-marriage. "Your grace, you are too kind."

"You must call me Taryn." Dropping one hand, the duchess turned to face the others. "And this is my dear friend, Kexen—Lady Tentrees—and Prince Ronan. By a happy coincidence, they are both visiting. Everyone is so relieved about the danger from the Swarm being neutralized that the king wanted to celebrate with his family around him."

Yes, Rory had heard of that particular danger. It had frightened everyone, even the baron. His own fears were too close and real for him to be concerned about anything so remote. Still, now that he was here with Evan, he was glad to know that there wasn't some foreign danger that would force Evan to leave him and fight.

Kexen stepped closer and dipped a curtesy. "It's lovely to meet you, Lady Windham. If this trend of male brides keeps up, the castle will be full of us."

"Yes," Prince Ronan agreed. "It's a shame that Carwyn and Cariad aren't able to join us with their husbands. They are relatives on the other side of our family and off keeping us safe. Still, I'm happy to meet you, Lady Windham, and delighted that your husband's return will give the gossips' tongues something new to wag about. My poor Jarl Tarben's ears have been burning with it since we arrived, although it doesn't seem to bother him. Very little does."

Rory swallowed hard as he absorbed all the information. "You will have to forgive me, but I've lived a rather sheltered life. I'm trying to catch up to the world around me."

"I'm sorry," the duchess said. "We can be a bit much. You must be tired…or hungry? Shall I order some tea?"

"Thank you, no. I've had plenty of that already." He patted his stomach, although it was really more full from nervousness than food. "Would it be possible for me to get some fresh air? I've gotten used to being outside these last few weeks." He didn't add that being inside a castle of any type reminded him of how he'd been effectively imprisoned in one his whole life.

"Of course, we'll go to the family's garden." Looping his arm around Rory's, Taryn led them all out into the corridor, down some steps and out into a lovely place with green grass, a riot of colorful flowers and a nicely appointed gazebo, to where they ventured. Once they'd all seated themselves on the plush cushions, the other three stared him with unabashed curiosity.

Rory clapped his hands to his cheeks. "What is it? Do I have something on my face?"

Prince Ronan laughed. "No, of course not. Please excuse our rudeness. There are so few of us male brides that we are fascinated by your arrival and want to learn everything there is to know about you." The others nodded in agreement. "I'm sure I speak for all of us when I ask you to tell us how your marriage came about. For us, you see, the circumstances weren't always as voluntary is one might wish. We're all deliriously happy now with our husbands, of course, but that wasn't always so. Were you forced into this?"

"Oh no!" Rory nearly laughed at the question. "Marrying Evan was the first decision about my life that I actually got to make myself. I'm right where I want to be, except I'm worried about Evan." He couldn't keep his thoughts about that to himself, and although he'd only just met these boys, he felt a kinship toward them. If there was anybody in the palace who would understand, he believed it was these young men, who were also brides of powerful men.

The Duchess of Vostguard reached over to pat his thigh. "Tell us whatever you want. I promise we are here to help you."

So he told them the whole tale, starting with his conception, relieved to be able to speak of it and feeling more relaxed with each word he got out.

* * * *

Evan wasn't happy to discover that Rory was not in the bed chamber assigned to them. Lady Clarissa had assured him that his wife was safe, visiting with family members. Still, he hated the fact that the boy wasn't within reach. There was no immediate danger, and none at all for his wife, but he'd become accustomed to being able to simply reach out and touch him. Except for the day of Rory's failed attempt at escape, they had never been so far apart since he'd kidnapped him. That beginning felt like eons ago. The shame of it was fresh, however, and he suspected it always would be.

He tried to sit and relax. With having vomited out to Nora everything that had led him to this point, his stomach wasn't so tied up in knots. To be honest, he hadn't known this much peace since he'd first discovered the baron's perfidy. He'd pretended that being a brigand was more a lark than anything fearful and had projected that confidence to the others. But it had been a lie. He'd lived with the bone-deep fear that he was leading others to their doom. With a possible path forward that would make his efforts moot, he could admit to himself that no matter what happened to him from this point, everyone would be better off without the stealing from the rich and giving to the poor. It was a solution to the problem that was always going to fall under its own weight. He wouldn't miss that larcenous life at all.

His belief could be laid squarely in Nora's reaction to hearing about how her bannerman taxed his people to the point of starvation to feed his own greed. She knew nothing about what he'd told her mother yet wasn't surprised to learn that Tost's review of the matter had yielded no positive results. The man, she had said, was a weasel of epic proportions who had rued the day he crossed her father by way of his wife. She would pursue the problem, starting with updating the king with the truth. It was her duty to take care of it. *"Trust me,"* she had said—and he did. They hadn't spoken about his fate, nor had he wanted to worry her on his account. It was enough that she would take care of Rory.

A timid knock had him straightening. "Come."

Maxwell entered, followed by Manfred and Nemo. The older servant took in the room with a sweep of his gaze. "Where is my master?"

"Visiting with the Duchess of Vostguard and others. He's fine. If I thought otherwise, I wouldn't be sitting here."

Maxwell grimaced, but otherwise said nothing.

Nemo pushed past him and made a circuit of the chamber, touching everything with their slender fingers. "I always figured nobility lived a nice life. I never imagined anything like this. Don't you worry about getting it dirty?"

Evan waved the question away. "No, because there's always more to replace it. And it's someone else's problem to worry about, in any event. I just get to sit on my fat ass and issue orders." He snorted. "Give me a pallet of ferns and a bower of branches and flowers any day. If not for Rory, I'd bed down with the palace guards. I've always felt more at home in a place like that than these precious spaces."

Manfred hummed. "Nice for you to make such a *sacrifice* for the boy, though. He deserves some pampering, Evan."

He opened his mouth to agree when his door swung open and four large men came barreling in. "This room is getting rather crowded." He stood, gesturing to his other guests to back away. He greeted the first man with a bow. "Your highness."

He knew Soren, of course, and the look on the man's face was not an encouraging one. His brother-by-marriage was a decent and affable man—unless you crossed him. And he had done so. There was no more ruthless person in Moorcondia than Soren with the right provocation. Evan wouldn't be surprised if this was his destiny entering the room.

The prince stood with arms crossed and legs braced. "Nora tells me I must forgive your treatment of this family these last few years. As Merida's widower, I'm disinclined, except she would want me to, as well." He threw up his hands. "Gods, Evander, why didn't you come to me directly the first time?"

"I went to my liege lady, as was proper." He dropped his gaze. "I will, however, always regret not pursuing the matter with her. I gave up too easily and should have known better. She wasn't one to let a bastard like Finley treat his people—and hers by extension—with such cruelty. For that poor judgment, I do humbly beg your forgiveness."

"You've always been a cocky son-of-a-bitch, too sure that you knew best and convinced you were the smartest person in the room, no matter the circumstances."

Evan couldn't help shrugging. "Well, in my own defense, I usually am." The breath got knocked out of him, and he grunted as Soren hugged him with rib-crushing strength and thumped him on the back.

"Damn if you're not right about that. You and your wife are welcome," the man said as he stood back. "I will go to the king with Nora to see what can be done about Finley. This time, we'll push for him to be summoned here instead of sending an emissary to him." He frowned. "I can't promise anything about how the king will deal with you, however."

"My fate is not your concern, your highness. As long as Rory is protected and provided for..."

"That goes without saying." Soren heaved a breath and clasped his hands behind him. "And as you have joined the ranks of men with boy brides, I thought you might like to meet these gentlemen." He gestured toward a man a little younger than he who had the fine looks and dress of a courtier. "This is Lord Benedict Tentrees."

The man sketched a bow and shot him a grin. "Lord Windham."

"Jarl Tarben is from the Dark Mountains and husband to Prince Ronan."

The largest of them all and rough looking, even in a well-cut and appointed tunic and trousers, nodded once with a shrewd look in his eyes, sizing Evan up. "A pleasure to meet you, my lord. With your arrival, no one seems interested in me anymore." He bared his teeth in what must pass as a smile among his wild people. "Thanks for that."

"And you know Sir Rolf, I believe."

"My lord." The man Evan thought of as Soren's shadow gave a quick bow and started to fade into the background.

A loud gasp had them all turning in Maxwell's direction. The old servant clutched at Manfred's sleeve as he stared wide-eyed at Rolf. "It's him." He shifted his gaze to Evan. "That's him, the knight."

"The knight?" The meaning hit Evan like a club. He took a step toward Rolf, his anger a hard thing to hold back. "You were Baroness Finley's lover once, were you not?" With the woman dead, there was no one else for him to direct his fury to. He despised men who bedded women, not caring what the night of pleasure might yield. That contempt held new meaning with his darling Rory's miserable childhood haunting his thoughts.

The knight looked at Soren and took a half-step back before stopping his feet and standing tall. "If by that, my lord, do you mean that the baroness ordered me to her bed while my former liege lord visited her husband, then yes. It is not a time of my life that I've thought about in years, and it certainly isn't a fond memory. Being made to service a noblewoman on pain of being falsely accused of forcing myself on her is not something I'm proud of or wish to revisit."

"He's right," Maxwell said in a low voice. "That is how it was. My lady was the center of my life, and I was honor bound to serve her. But she was a selfish person and thought only of her own pleasure. It didn't matter if this good knight was willing or not. She wanted him, and that was enough."

Rolf's eyes narrowed. "I know you. Always standing behind her and lurking in the shadows of her chamber." He looked at Evan. "What is this all about, my lord?"

Soren put his hands on his hips. "Yes, what?"

Evan wasn't sure how to answer. Rory might not appreciate his spilling his secrets without clearing it with him first. It wasn't his tale to tell, after all. *Fuck it.* As the boy's husband, it was his duty to protect him from everything, even heartache and embarrassment.

He studied the knight. "Does red hair run in your family, Sir Rolf."

Obviously surprised at the question, the man nevertheless answered, as he'd been trained to do with someone of authority. "As it happens, it does. If you saw a gathering of them, my lord, you'd wonder what dull shrubbery my parents found me under. If I didn't bear such a strong resemblance to my father, he might worry about the origin of my birth." He ended with a quick smile to indicate that wasn't really a concern. "Why do you ask?"

"Because my wife, Rory Finley, born eighteen years ago, has a beautiful head of hair the color of a sunset." There was silence then, the kind that one might describe as 'thundering'.

Sir Rolf's chest heaved before he cried out and punched the door behind him. Soren went to him and tried to touch his shoulder, but the man brushed him off. "Do not dare to try to comfort me, your grace." He turned with burning eyes. "You know that I've never married and have been careful not to father children outside of that commitment. A soldier can make for a poor family man, and I would never disrespect a woman by leaving her with my seed growing inside her—nor would I leave a child wanting from the lack of support of their father. I had no thought of this outcome and was only relieved to escape her clutches."

"Finley knew, didn't he?" There was anguish in his tone.

It was Maxwell who answered before Evan could. "Yes."

"And the baron made his life a misery because of it, yet not having the balls to decree him a bastard and send him to his mother's family." It wasn't a question.

Maxwell answered anyway. "Yes. She shielded the boy from the worst of it. When she died…" He shook his head.

"Where is he?" Rolf demanded of Evan. "Where is my son?"

Soren took his man by the arm, not allowing him to shake him off. "Rolf, you must settle down before you see him. Your fury is understandable but it's the boy who matters now. Although I hope he will accept you as his father, he must not be pressured to do so. And we must let his husband break this news to him and decide what's best."

Rolf's glare at Evan was incendiary. "Did you force him into it? The marriage, I mean."

"No." As hard as it was, Evan made himself to look the man in the eye. "I didn't always do right by him, but this marriage is intended to protect him. Finley has no more power over the boy as long as he's my wife—and even if he becomes my widow," he added with a mutter.

"That can always be arranged." Rolf's expression lent credence to his threat.

Soren shook him gently. "Rolf, this isn't helping. Let us take a ride before supper. It will clear your head, and if you want someone to hit afterward, I'm sure the jarl will oblige."

The big man laughed and flexed a fist. "Always happy to. I didn't have a chance to fuck my wife this morning, so I have some energy to burn myself."

Soren made a sound like a growling bear. "Must you always provoke me so?"

"So long as your reaction rewards me, yes."

Rolf interceded. "Thank you, your grace. A ride would be most welcome. I can do without the fistfight, though...probably." He glared at Evan. "I will accede to your authority as a husband, but know this, my lord—I will gut you like a deer if you hurt my son."

Evan nodded once. "That's fair."

Chapter Ten

"You don't have to be so careful, Evan."

Sweat dripped down his face and every muscle strained with the effort to stay still. His cock was embedded up to the hilt in Rory's tight, silky ass. His channel worked Evan's dick with undulating waves that the boy was probably unaware of. Because this was only the second time he'd mounted his wife, he knew he was causing at least discomfort, if not pain. He needed to be sure that the boy was sufficiently acclimated to the invasion before thrusting.

But his stubborn wife had other ideas. He wrapped both legs around Evan's waist and smacked one heel against his cheek. "Fuck me, Evan. Please. I want to feel every inch of you, and you've already made me come twice. It's your turn now."

As strong as he was, Evan was unable to resist the lure of the wet sheath encasing his cock and the need for his balls to empty. He tried a tentative thrust, and when Rory's face showed no sign of hurt, he slowly picked up speed. The moment the boy bucked his hips to meet him, he let loose. Hard and fast, he drove himself into his wife, leveraging himself with his hands on either side of his head. He felt the moment when Rory climaxed again, his hole clamping down on his dick. His seed poured out of him, robbing him of his coherent thought and making his muscles weak. He collapsed on top of his wife, panting and shuddering.

Rory traced slender fingers along his back, murmuring his appreciation. When Evan had the good sense to try to stop squishing the boy, he held him fast. "Stay. I like the feel of you pressing down on me."

"I shall crush you, darling."

"Hardly. This mattress is so soft that it's like falling into a cloud." His hole spasmed. "If I keep you inside me, will you get hard again and fuck me some more?"

Evan groaned and found the energy to kiss him. He loved exploring his wife's mouth with his tongue. Every part of him was soft, sweet and enticing. Spending the night just like this was very appealing. As long as they were secluded in their chamber, they could pretend that the rest of the world didn't exist. They'd been spared having an audience with the king or having to dine with the rest of the court. Instead, Soren had treated them to a quiet family dinner in his quarters. His nieces were delightful, so like their mother. It made him sad and happy at the same time. He missed his sister yet could take comfort in her daughters. And they'd been so kind to Rory, especially Taryn. With such a powerful man to ease him into the life of a nobleman's wife, Rory would be fine. Evan didn't need to worry about him much.

Of course, he did. The baron would come within the week, and while he didn't doubt the man would get his comeuppance, it also meant that he himself would be next in line to face the king's ire. But he wasn't going to let those worrisome thoughts cloud this time he had with his wife. He wanted to make memories with Rory, the kind that could sustain them both, whatever came. So he kissed and petted and enjoyed as much as he could reach and naturally, his dick hardened again.

This time, he fucked long and slow, making the pleasure last. He wanted to whisper into Rory's ear, as well, tell him…what? That he adored him, desired him? His body conveyed those feelings. It was the words that stuck in his throat. With his future uncertain, that was nothing he dared feel, let alone say. For now, he'd let his cock do his talking for him.

* * * *

Rory was spent and a little sore, but not so much that he didn't consider waking his husband to seduce him into another mounting. The man slept like the dead, his handsome face relaxed as it typically never was. Being in the palace, he must feel safe enough to let go of his worries. As much as he enjoyed his new-found pleasure, it wouldn't be kind of him to wake the man.

"Is there something you want to ask me, wife?"

Rory rolled his eyes. "I didn't move a muscle or make a sound. How did I wake you, and how do you know what I'm thinking?"

Evan snaked a hand around his waist and tugged him so that they were face-to-face. "My cock sensed it, I suppose, and woke me like a claxon."

Rory wiggled his hand between them and wrapped his fingers around the hard cock he found. "I wouldn't want to disappoint it." He loved the low moan Evan made. Before he could do more, however, his husband pulled his hand away. "What's the matter? Did I hurt you?" His husband had been so ruthlessly effective at bringing him pleasure, he hadn't had time to learn any skills.

Evan kissed the hand and sat up. "You could never do that. Your every touch is a balm to my heart and a boon to my desires. I need to speak with you about something."

Alarm shot through him. Rory sat bolt upright and bit back a mewl of distress. "What is it?"

Evan cursed. "Calm yourself, wife. I'm sorry I'm doing a bad job of this already. Nothing is wrong. In fact," he added with a jerk of his head, "it might be good news."

Life's hard lessons made him doubt that, however much he trusted this man. "Just say it, Evan."

"Very well." Evan took both of Rory's hands in his own. "I have found your father. The knight who lay with your mother, that is, and made you."

This was not what he had been expecting. His mind had been on the baron and his unknown fate tied to a brigand. He never thought about this nameless and faceless man who'd planted his seed inside his mother. It didn't matter, because the knowledge wasn't going to change his life. He swallowed hard a few times and drew in deep breaths to calm himself.

"Who is it?"

"His name is Sir Rolf, and he's Soren's man. Maxwell recognized him when the prince came to speak with me this afternoon. He didn't know, Rory."

"You mean he didn't care to know." He couldn't keep the bitterness out of his voice.

"He was young, darling, no older than you are now, I imagine. I think what happened to him was traumatic.

Your mother didn't seduce him. She coerced him. He was furious to learn that he had a son living with the terror of the baron. He wants to meet you."

Rory shook his head and tugging his hands free, practically tumbled from the bed. He paced, absorbing the information and trying to work out how he felt about it all. His mind was reeling. He'd hated the knight for so long, making him into a villain along with his mother and Maxwell. If he'd thought about it, he would have expected the man to be older, someone happy to take a bit of fun with his host's wife. A young, vulnerable boy didn't fit with that narrative.

He wrung his hands. "Am I supposed to feel sorry for him?"

"There is no 'supposed to' in this, darling. However you feel is the right way, and you must know I support whatever decision you make. I will not allow him to come near you if that is what you want."

"Oh, I don't know!" He couldn't keep the tears from falling. The next thing he knew he was wrapped in Evan's strong arms, being rocked and soothed like a baby, except he wasn't sure anyone had ever bothered to do that for him. *Evan does. He always will.* He felt it then, like a thunderbolt to his heart. *I love him.* Silly to fall so for someone he barely knew. It didn't make it any less true, though.

He clung to his husband and dried up his own tears. Crying never solved anything and left him feeling hollow. "I don't know what to do with this knowledge. Does he have red hair?" Not that such a fact made any difference, but it was the one thing that had announced his bastardry to all and sundry.

"It runs in his family, apparently, but no, his is a rather ordinary brown."

"I need time to think about it."

"Of course you do. Come to bed now. The sun isn't even up yet."

"Will you fuck me again."

"Darling, you only need to ask."

* * * *

As usual, Rory clutched his husband's hand, taking comfort in his strength. "It is strange that I feel both excitement and fear? I want to see the baron being punished, but the thought of seeing him again makes my blood freeze."

"He won't get anywhere near you. And we can leave anytime you want."

Rory wasn't sure that was true. While they stood to the side, out of the king's line of sight, he didn't think the man would appreciate someone leaving a court hearing without permission. Thank the gods the king hadn't summoned them yet to give account of themselves. Every communication had been conveyed by Nora, Prince Soren and various ministers. One of them, a kindly old man, had quizzed him for a long time on what life with the baron had been like. It wasn't his personal grievances that mattered. The minister asked many questions about the baron's lifestyle. Rory didn't know much about how the baron ran his corner of the world, but he'd seen for himself how opulent the man lived. And with Evan filling in the unknown parts about the state of the peasants, it was easy to see how the taxes had been levied to a harsh degree for the baron's own riches.

The herald sounded the baron's arrival. The murmurs of the courtiers died down and everyone looked to the entrance to the throne room. Rory couldn't hold back the sharp breath and the nervous shock in seeing the man who had effectively tortured him his whole life. Evan was there, soothing him with gentle strokes along his back. He forced himself to relax and focus on the spectacle to come. From what his husband had conveyed, the baron wasn't going to wiggle out of his trouble. It wasn't only peasants he'd wronged.

The baron swaggered in, his fawning retinue of men trailing behind him. He approached the king's dais and bowed low. "Your majesty, I am honored by your summons and surprised by it." His expression was cheerful, but no one should be fooled by that. His jaw was tight with anger.

"You shouldn't be," the king said, then waved at Princess Eleanora, who sat to one side.

She was not much older than Rory, yet she held herself with admirably regal confidence. "Baron Finley."

The man swept another bow. "Your grace, I don't believe I've had the pleasure of meeting you until now."

"You'll want to guard your pretty words, my lord, until you've heard why I asked the king to bring you to me."

"I am at your service, your grace."

Having spent a lifetime studying the man for signs of anger, Rory wasn't deceived by his easy tone and relaxed stance. "He's mad," he whispered to his husband.

Evan leaned down to speak in his ear. "Trust my niece and the king. They are not idiots."

Nora opened a book she carried and stared at some pages. "My accounts for your lands seem to be out of sorts with your collections."

The baron spread his hands wide. "I'm sorry, your grace, but I can assure you I pay what I owe."

"Indeed?" The woman raised her eyebrows. "I sent men ahead of your summons to speak with the leaders of some of your villages and towns. What they say about the taxes you collect, along with the testimony of my uncle, lead me to believe otherwise."

"Your grace, those peasants are constant troublemakers. You can't trust what they say, and I'm sorry but I don't know your uncle."

Nora pointed in Evan's direction and naturally it meant that the baron's gaze tracked her fingers. He frowned in obvious confusion when he spied Evan. Of course, he'd never seen the brigand who held mastery over his roads. But he soon caught sight of someone he did know. Rory whimpered and pressed against Evan's chest.

"I'm sorry, darling. I didn't realize she would draw attention to us."

"Rory! What is my wayward son doing here?" he foolishly demanded of the duchess. Then he immediately changed demeanor because he wasn't entirely stupid. "I mean to say, my dear son was kidnapped. I thought he was lost to me." He turned his attention to the king. "Your majesty, I humbly beg your forgiveness, but I've been mourning the death of a son who has all along been in the clutches of your niece's uncle. I can't tell you how overjoyed I am to find him safe."

He made to take a step in Rory's direction. And although he couldn't help shrinking closer to Evan, he also chose in that moment to stand defiant. He'd always hidden his fear as much as possible. Now more than ever, he had the power to be confident.

Nora stopped the man with a chilling voice. "I'm sure you are very surprised to find Rory alive and well, given that you refused to pay the ransom."

"No, your grace. That's not true."

"Don't lie to me."

The baron drew himself up straight. "I was never given the chance to pay the ransom. His being here proves that. And your accounts are wrong, your grace. They are tricky things to manage and beneath your notice. Perhaps if you would allow my bookkeeper to lend you a hand with them..."

The king made everyone jump by pounding on his arm rest. "Never question my niece's skill with numbers. She says they don't add up, so explain yourself, baron. What have you done with the coin you've been squeezing out of the people you are supposed to be protecting?"

"I...I can't say, your majesty. I am not as good with math as the duchess obviously is." He gave a guileless smile. "I trust others too much, it seems. My tax collector may have betrayed me. That's the only explanation that I have. I would welcome some help."

"He's lying," Rory bit out.

"Everyone knows that, darling."

Rory wasn't so sure. The man was cunning and could be very persuasive when he wanted to be. At least he was being called out on cheating the duchess. It had never occurred to him that the baron was doing that, and it made for a stronger desire to punish him than merely hurting some peasants.

Nora looked down her nose at him. "If it's help that you need, then that is what you'll get. I will install my own bookkeeper, among others, to get you on the right path and keep you there. People should not be taxed to the point of starvation, and I insist on getting my fair share, as well. I will not tolerate any more of this *mistake*." Her warning was clear. The days of the baron's stealing from everyone were over.

The baron bowed low. "I assure you it won't happen again, your grace. Your understanding and patience in this matter are greatly appreciated." He licked his lips before turning to stare Rory right in the eye. The gaze was like daggers shooting at him. "And I will gladly take my son back home where he belongs—at Finley Keep."

"Not anymore he doesn't," the king bit out. "He's Lady Evander Windham now and under the protection of his husband."

It was almost comical to watch the baron's mouth open and close before he could sputter out a response. "That's ridiculous. They're both men."

The king cocked his head. "Your point being?"

"It's not a true union. For that, one needs a man and a woman."

"Are you saying that my brother's marriage is also not real? And my son's, as well?"

"No, no, your majesty, of course not. But those are political alliances—treaties, a necessary contrivance to achieve an important goal. Rory is no one of importance. He's not even my heir and comes with nothing of value to recommend him."

The king smiled in a way that would freeze a wise person's blood. "I'm sure his husband would disagree with that assessment of his bride. Are you challenging the validity of the marriage? I've been assured it's been consummated, if that's your concern."

The baron's expression would have been comical if the man weren't so hateful. "Not at all. It's merely such a shocking surprise. I never gave my approval for the marriage or negotiated a contract, for that matter. A father has certain rights," he added with a firm nod.

"Yes, he does!" a voice rang out. Through the crowd, the knight that Evander had pointed out as Rory's true sire pushed to stand near the baron. "But you are not Rory's father. I am. And it's past time for that fact to be recognized by one and all. Your pardon, your majesty," the man added with a bow.

The baron's face turned bright red. "What madness is this? I don't know this man."

"No, you wouldn't remember me or my brief visit to your castle, but I do. You're a venal brute of a man. I would have felt sorry for your baroness if she hadn't preyed on me herself. I never knew about the boy. Now that I do, I will *not* let you claim him as your son any longer, nor will I tolerate your cruelty to him."

The baron backed up and pointed a finger at the knight. "He's lying. My dear, late wife would never have lain with him…unless he forced her."

Rory's stomach dropped at the accusation, knowing it was false. He started forward to speak in the man's defense, except Evander held him back.

"He doesn't need your help, darling. Sir Rolf is held in high esteem in this court. No one would believe such an accusation against him, least of all Prince Soren, and he has the king's ear. The baron doesn't understand anything about this court or how vulnerable he is away from his own domain."

Rolf took a step toward the baron, his hand on the hilt of his sword. "If it's a challenge for the truth you seek, I am ready to meet it here and now." He sneered at the man as his gaze raked him from head to toe. "I assume you will pick a champion to fight in your stead."

The baron looked back at his captain of the arms who'd stuck by his side as he'd always done. Rory knew firsthand how much the man enjoyed doing the baron's dirty work for him. Not this time, however. Rory knew a moment of great satisfaction when the man took a step back. Clearly his loyalty to his liege lord had limits, and given the size of Sir Rolf and the furious gleam in his eyes, only a fool or a madman would have agreed to face him in personal combat.

The baron huffed with quiet outrage. "Your majesty, are you going to permit this scoundrel to threaten me, a guest of your court?"

The king flicked his hand. "This is a matter of honor. The crown will be satisfied with whatever outcome occurs."

For long seconds, no one said anything. Rory almost felt sorry for the man he'd called 'father' his whole life. He was truly in a trouble of his own making. It should have been a satisfying moment for him, but as much as he would have liked to think so, he simply wasn't as blood thirsty as the baron had tried to raise him to be. There was nothing he could do, however. He was smart enough to know that he had no say in any of this. Powerful men would decide his fate, as usual. For the first time, however, he felt secure, no matter the outcome, because Evan was there to protect him.

The tension broke when Prince Soren left his place on the dais and stepped between his man and the baron. "Gentleman, I think we can all agree that bloodshed serves no purpose. A simple apology seems in order. Don't you agree, Sir Rolf?"

"Yes, your grace." The man removed his hand from his sword hilt, the effort to do so clearly showing on his face and in the way he stood.

The prince turned to the baron. "And you, my lord?"

The baron didn't hesitate to nod. "Yes, of course. I beg your pardon, Sir Rolf. I spoke in haste. You are obviously a man of honor, and you are welcome to the brat if that is what you wish. He makes for a terrible son. You'll see."

Sir Rolf took a sudden step toward the man with his teeth bared. The baron jumped back and made a sound much like a squeal.

The sight of it made Rory smile. "He can't hurt me anymore."

Evan squeezed him tightly. "No, never again."

All tension left Rory's body as the baron made his escape from the king's scrutiny. *It's over.* He'd forgotten, however, that one must always be on guard for trouble, making it that much harder to swallow when it came roaring back to punch him in the gut.

"Now to the next order of business." The king stared directly at them, proving that he'd known where they were all along. "Evander, Lord Windham, step forward."

Chapter Eleven

Evan tried to shake his wife as he went before the king. The damn boy clung to him like moss to a tree, forcing him to bring Rory along. He wouldn't even let go of Evan's hand as they made their bows. As a show of loyalty, it was humbling. But the husband in him was desperate to separate Rory from the bad that was coming—not that he worried the boy would be held responsible for Evan's transgressions. Still, what was about to transpire would frighten him, he was sure. He understood that Rory had come to depend on him for safety. No amount of reassurance was going to make him truly believe that as Evan's wife, he was free of the baron and could live a life of freedom and security. He tried to keep him calm by squeezing his hand as they waited for the king to speak.

The man was a master at making one sweat. He stared long and hard at Evan, drumming his fingers on the armrest of his throne. "Congratulations, my lord. You are a case of first impression for this court—maybe for any in the world—a nobleman who has committed ignoble crimes but for a noble purpose. What to do with you, hmm?"

"If I may speak, your majesty?" When the king waved him ahead, he said the words he'd practiced silently on his journey to the capital. "I offer no excuse for my actions and take full responsibility for them. I and I alone am responsible for the band of brigands robbing people for the riches they gained through supporting the baron's actions, however indirectly. As my brother-by-marriage recently reminded me, I've always been arrogant, sure of the rightness of my actions and that I had the answer to any problem.

"I cannot regret helping those in need. My men and I kept countless people, especially children, from starving in the winter months. For that, I make no apology. But I should have trusted in those higher than me to address the problem rather than taking matters into my own hands. I've thought long and hard about this and realized that what I did was out of guilt, as well. If I hadn't been so selfish, so determined to travel as I pleased, and had remained instead as my sister's castellan, I could have prevented the baron from preying on his people." He took a deep breath and let it out slowly. "I stand ready to accept whatever punishment you see fit to impose."

The king rubbed his finger along his chin, his expression giving nothing away. "Very pretty words, my lord. And I gauge them sincere, as well, and don't discount that fact. But highway robbery is only one step away from murder. The people you robbed were rich, yes. Still, most brigands are not as…selective. Stealing people's money in other circumstances can lead to the very starvation problem that you say you wanted to solve. Do you think the average citizens would see the distinction? What kind of message am I sending to my people if I bend the rules for a nobleman—one who is also related to me by marriage—when anyone else in your predicament would see the rest of his life spent in the mines?"

Rory squeezed his hand with sufficient force to break a bone. Although his instinct was to comfort his wife, Evan had no choice except to keep his focus on the king. "I expect no special treatment, your majesty. You are a just king, and your punishment will be, as well."

"If any other man said that, I would think they were buttering me up for leniency, but you are honorable and have no guile. I must think on this. In the meantime, you will be locked up as anyone else who stands accused of a crime would be." He gestured to soldiers stationed to the side.

Rory grabbed Evan's hand with his other one, as if to anchor him to the spot. "No." The word was issued more as a plea than as a command.

It broke Evan's heart to see his wife in such distress, but so far the king was placing blame squarely on him. Nothing could change that and risk Rory's new-found freedom. The boy was blameless in any event.

Evan looked to Rolf as the soldiers started a tug-of-war with his other arm. "Please, take him."

The man didn't have to be asked twice. Grabbing Rory by the wrists, he broke his hold of Evan and pulled him away. When the boy struggled in earnest to get back to him, the knight simply wrapped his arm around Rory's waist and carted him away. Evan waited until his wife's protests had faded away before bowing to the king and allowing himself to be removed with as much grace as he could muster.

* * * *

The king had a very modern dungeon. Instead of dank stone cells with small, barred windows, it had steel cages with three open sides. One could see a great deal around them, which obviously meant the guards had a good view of their prisoners at all times. There would be no nighttime digging at the back wall to make an escape, not that he intended to do any such thing. His only hope was that the king would be merciful enough to sentence him to long years in the mines with a chance to be released before he turned old and gray. And as long as Rory got to live a comfortable life on his own terms, that would be a good outcome, regardless. It was hard at the moment, though, to be cooped up after living outdoors for so many years.

As he paced his cell, a bit of a commotion caught his attention. His heart sank as he saw two guards muscling Nemo down the corridor. They shot Evan a smile as the guards shoved them into the cell next door and clanged the door shut behind them. Nemo simply waved a good-bye at them with a cocky smile. One of the guards sported a black eye and snarled at Nemo as he stalked away.

Evan grabbed the bars their cells shared and sighed at Nemo. "I should have insisted that you leave before entering the palace."

Nemo said nothing. They made a turn of their small cell first before stopping in front of Evan. "You don't honestly think I'm here because the king ordered it, do you? How insulting. As if I'd let them capture me." They shrugged. "I picked a fight with one of the guards so that they'd arrest me."

Evan couldn't help grinning. "I saw you got a good lick in."

"He had a face like a pillow. The king keeps a very clean dungeon. The rushes are fresh." They walked over to the pallet and stretched out on it, hands behind their head. "Softer than what we're used to. And it doesn't come with a gaggle of servants clucking like hens while I'm trying to sleep. I don't know how Maxwell stands it."

Evan gripped the bars. "Where is he?"

"With your lady love, where else?"

Evan almost said Rory was no such thing, but he wasn't entirely sure that was true. Technically the boy was a lady, and if Evan peered into his own self hard enough, he suspected he'd find that he was his love, too. *No, don't think such things. There is no future for you.* "Why did you connive your way in here? You aren't planning on helping me escape?"

"No. I don't fancy our chances on that. I thought you might like the company."

Evan grimaced. "So long as you don't plan on following me to the mines." The very thought of anyone else suffering for his sins was intolerable. When Nemo said nothing, he changed the topic. "Where is Manfred?"

"He's with the local abbot, a decent sort of man who Manfred hopes will hear him out about the brutality visited upon the initiates and the local boys by his old order. Apparently rape, torture and slavery are not basic tenants of the church."

Evan dropped his hands. "That's good. If nothing else, he should have the protection of this local abbot." He went to lie on his own pallet. It really was surprisingly comfortable. *Maybe the mines won't be so bad, either.* It didn't matter, anyway. It was Rory who preyed on his mind. He had to believe that Maxwell and Rolf and the rest of Merida's family had the boy well in hand.

* * * *

"Get out!" Rory grabbed a nearby bowl and heaved it in Maxwell's direction. It smashed against the wall as the old man had learned over the years to be nimble. "I told you I don't want your help. Just leave me alone!" He bit back a sob and wrapped his arms around his waist.

This room that he'd shared with his husband had become his prison—not that he was being forced to stay there. It was simply that he didn't want to go anywhere or see anyone, other than Evan, and that wasn't going to happen any time soon...perhaps never. The king was pondering Evan's fate at that very moment and had refused Rory's plea to be heard. He had no doubt that at any moment, he'd get word that his husband had been carted off to the mines, never to be seen again. The thought of it was unbearable. *I wish I never met him. Life or death with the baron would have been preferable.* But for Evan, he wouldn't have ever known a better life than the one he'd had, and this new pain of being separated from the man he loved was far crueler than anything the baron had ever done to him.

The only place to vent his spleen was the same one he'd used since his mother had died. Only the thought of how disappointed Evan would be in him kept him from throwing something else at his old servant. "Go back to the woods and find Maurice. He seems taken with your boney ass. I'm sure life with him will be better than it has been with me."

Maxwell said nothing, merely stared at him with a disapproving look. No, that wasn't entirely true. There was something else in the man's eyes...pity. That was worse because it made it harder for Rory to hold back his tears. He picked up a candle stick and raised his arm. He'd drive the old man away, a better outcome for both of them. The door swung open, startling him, although Maxwell didn't seem surprised.

Sir Rolf strode in. "Put that down! Leave us," he added with barely a glance at Maxwell.

The servant was out of the door, shutting it behind him before Rory could object. Although he'd wanted the man gone, he was preferable to this stranger about whom Rory was unsure of his feelings. As with Evander, the risk to his heart was too great to form any attachment to the man, regardless of how he'd stood up to the baron.

Rory put the candlestick back on the table with a thump. "What are *you* doing here?"

"I was patient and gave you the space that Lord Windham insisted, but now is the time for me to act as your father." He took a step closer, his expression softening. "I promise I will keep you safe from the baron. He won't menace you ever again."

Rory turned away. "I don't care about that. I only want Evan to be set free."

"Of that, I have no news and cannot offer you reassurance. The king is a fair man, but he has to do what's best for Moorcondia at large. The fate of one man cannot take precedence."

Rory wheeled around to face him. "I don't give a damn about Moorcondia. All that matters to me is Evan. He holds my heart in his hand, and it's breaking. He should never have stolen me or it. I was better off when it was a hard, brittle lump of nothing. Why did he give me hope when he must have known all along that he was doomed by coming here?"

To his mortification, he could no longer hold back the tears. As if a dam burst, they flooded out of his eyes and down his cheeks. He fell to the floor on a sob, cradling his own waist to keep his insides from bursting out. As he cried, he rocked to soothe himself as he hadn't done since he'd been a very young child. Everything was impossibly bleak, and he didn't think he had the strength to go on.

Strong arms embraced him and held him tight. At first, Rory struggled to break free, but this man who was his true father wouldn't let him. He murmured soothing words as he let Rory cry himself dry.

He hiccupped now with every breath, struggling to regain control. It was impossible. Instead, he snuggled into Rolf's embrace and poured his heart out. "I don't remember ever not being scared. My mother was my protector, but even she was dangerous to me. Sometimes I caught her looking at me with a hatred in her eyes that made me fear she would kill me herself. I never knew what to expect each day that I woke. The both of them—her and the baron after she was gone—treated me as their toy. On good days, I was ignored. On bad ones…"

Twisting his fingers past the collar of his tunic, he pulled out the pendant he always wore. "This was the one thing she ever gave me—and only because she was dying. I should have thrown it into the lake yet couldn't bring myself to do so. I don't know why I hold onto it."

"Because she was your mother and whatever her faults, she managed to think of giving you something of herself. It is perhaps the one bit of kindness in an otherwise horrible upbringing."

"I suppose you're right. But Evan has given me more in a few weeks than she ever did." He shook his head and buried his face in the warmth of a man who was as strong as Evan but didn't provide the same comfort as he did. He should have grown up with the surety of this place of safety and consolation. But many didn't, and he shouldn't feel so sorry for himself. He was nothing special...except Evan had made him feel that he was.

He clawed at Rolf's tunic. "Why did he give me hope? He should never have taken me, and once he did, he should have let me run as I had tried. I probably wouldn't have survived out there on my own, but at least I would have never known this horrible feeling. He made me feel for the first time and gave me pleasure that I didn't even dare dream about. How am I to live if he's not with me? Who will hold me at night and make me feel worthy?"

Rolf pulled him gently away to look him in the eye. "I'm sorry...for so many things. I have no answer to give you, except to say that I shall be grateful for the rest of my days that Lord Evander brought me to you. Your death would have been the worst possible outcome, so no more talk of that. The solace you get from your husband is beyond my power, but I will take care of you in all other ways. You are not alone anymore, my dear son, with only an aging servant to rely on. You have family and means to live your life, no matter what happens to Evander. So no more talk of how you aren't worthy. And please tell me what I can do for you now."

Rory grasped the man's arm. "I want Evander, to see him. Can you do that for me...father?"

Rolf pushed back strands of Rory's damp hair. "I am not without influence among the palace guards. I will take you to him."

* * * *

Evander was back to pacing his cell. He couldn't imagine how Nemo managed to be so relaxed, although he had to admit that he took solace from their presence, even if they said nothing.

Footsteps had him looking down the corridor and what he saw caused his heart to sink. Rory, accompanied by Sir Rolf, raced to his cell. His beautiful eyes were red from obvious crying. The sight of his wife's misery hurt as if he'd been punched in the chest. He had to stop himself from rubbing it for comfort.

"What are you doing here?" He hadn't meant to use a biting tone, but he realized as soon as the words were out of his mouth, that it was all for the best.

Rory looked taken aback for a second before giving him a trembling smile. "I was worried about you. Sir Rolf was kind enough to arrange for me to visit. How are you?" he added, clasping the bars.

"I'm fine," he replied brusquely. "The king keeps his prisoners in good conditions, as you can see. I've been given a nice, if boring, meal as well. Of course, the torture could start at any moment, so…." His words had the desired effect.

"Don't say such things! Surely the king won't do that."

Evan forced cocky grin. "Of course not. I was merely jesting to pass the time."

"It was *not* funny. Sir Rolf says that Prince Soren is lobbying the king on your behalf. You may still avoid a sentence to the mines."

Evan waved that away and walked to the back wall, where he lounged against it. "He feels he owes my dead sister that courtesy. Sentimental fool."

"Well, I for one am hopeful." Rory's expression had turned mad, and that was all to the good.

"It doesn't matter. At least at the mines, I will have hard labor to distract me and no responsibility for anyone else. It will make for a nice change. And really, what more could I want, given that I chose to live rough in the woods?"

Rory pressed his face against the bars. "Me. You'll have me, husband, if you are set free."

Evan made himself look indifferent. "That is sweet of you, darling, but I dare say there will be plenty of ripe pieces of ass at the mines to keep me company at night. And you will be free to seek your pleasure with others. With your face, wealth and status, you'll have no end of choices of eager men."

"I don't want anyone else." Rory's voice was tinged with tears now.

He had to harden his heart. This was what was best for the boy. After taking his freedom and his virginity, he owed Rory this much, at least. "You'll change your mind as the nights get long and that big bed feels empty. You're an eager and adventurous bedmate, Rory. I wish you well, and really there is no reason for you to pine after me. Frankly, you're lucky. I became a brigand because of the kind of man I *am*, not despite it."

Rory shook his head. "No, Evan, you don't understand. I love you!"

He would have thought himself too jaded to be moved by such a declaration. As it was, the knowledge that his wife felt that way made it easier for him to do what he must. "You are young and a bit foolish, boy. You have no idea what you are talking about. Just because I'm the first man who didn't treat you cruelly doesn't mean you have to love me. Such nonsense." He made himself look away from his wife's stunned face and focused his gaze on Sir Rolf. "Really, sir, you continue to be a poor father by letting your son stay down here, no matter how clean it is."

There was understanding in the man's eyes. "He's right. Come now, Rory. I've given you what you asked for. It's time to go back to where you belong."

Rory didn't allow himself to be tugged away from the bars right away. Tears welled up in his eyes yet didn't fall. The boy sniffed them back, and with a last, hurt look at Evan, he finally turned and left.

Evan closed his eyes and listened to the sound of his wife's footsteps as they faded away. He glanced at Nemo, who watched him with their usual keenness. "Shut up."

"I didn't say anything."

"I know what I'm doing."

"No one said you didn't. Idiot," they added under their breath.

Evan flopped down on his pallet. This was the right thing to do. Rory was finally free of the prison his parents had made for him. The king's decision was a foregone conclusion. Any hope to the contrary would lead to more heartache. Only one of them needed to suffer, and as Rory's husband, it was Evan's duty to be that one.

Chapter Twelve

"I told you I'm not interested in eating anything right now."

Maxwell hovered nearby, his silence a shouting condemnation of Rory's behavior, as if a good meal would solve everything. At least Rory didn't have the urge to throw anything. His crying jag with his father had purged a lifetime of fear and grief. It had left him feeling hollowed out, but that had been nothing compared to the emptiness left inside him when his husband had dismissed him from the dungeon...and his life. He'd returned to his room feeling eviscerated and insubstantial, as if he could simply float away and disappear. That had changed, though. Now he was just mad. *What makes him think he can cast me aside so easily?*

A simple rap on his door led to it being opened and in strode the Duchess of Vostguard, Prince Ronan and Lady Tentrees. *Why can't everyone leave me alone?* In his old life with the baron, that was often exactly what the castle inhabitants did. Now that he was related by marriage to the royal family, those old expectations didn't apply. He suppressed a sigh as he rose and made a bow. No matter how he felt, he was in no position to be rude to the prince and duchess, and although he believed he was of higher status than Lady Tentrees, courtesy cost him nothing.

He gestured toward the sitting area. "Welcome, gentlemen. Please be seated. Maxwell, bring refreshments for my guests."

"No need to bother," the duchess said. "But please give us some privacy." As soon as Maxwell had shut the door behind him, the duchess gave Rory a sympathetic look. "I won't ask you how you're feeling. We all know what it's like to worry about a husband."

Putting his chin on his palm, Rory said, "I don't know why I bother. He's made it clear he doesn't care if he spends his life with me or not." He straightened when the other boys laughed. "What?"

"Why ever would you think that?" Lady Tentrees asked.

"Because he told me so!"

That made the others laugh even more. The duchess shook his head. "You can't believe what he says."

"I can't?"

"Not on this particular topic. Men can be very stupid when it comes to tender feelings. Dumb things come out of their mouths that you simply have to take no notice of."

"But we're men. I don't lie about such things—although truth be told, before Evan, I had no cause to feel this way."

"I've seen the way he looks at you. His love is right there for all to notice if they look hard enough. Even Soren has remarked on it, and he's as blockheaded as the next man."

"You think so?" It was hard not to let his hopes rise once more.

"Absolutely." The other two nodded in agreement.

"He was so convincing when he told me he didn't care." He rubbed his palm over his heart. "It hurts."

"Of course it does," Lady Tentrees said. "And we aren't the same kind of men as our husbands. They think they have to be stoic all the time, noble in their protection of us."

"And treat us like we're as fragile as spun glass," the prince added. "Always protecting us, whether we need it or not. It's quite maddening," he added with a shake of his head.

The others did the same. Then the duchess slapped his thigh. "But we're stronger than they think and perfectly capable of finding a way out of a mess."

"I'm not as clever apparently, because I can't figure out how to get him released from that dungeon. The king denied my request to speak with him."

The prince rolled his eyes. "Oh, you can't rely on his help. He's the worst of the lot. Only in his case, it's as if the entire kingdom is his wife. He'll do what he thinks is for the greater good, no matter what his personal feelings are on the matter."

"I don't think he cares about sparing Evan."

The duchess leaned forward to pat Rory on the knee. "He does care. I know because Soren has told me as much. But my husband's sway over the king is limited. They are brothers, but as the older one, the king does not give his younger brother as much credence as he might."

Rory's stomach dropped. "Then there is no hope. If the king won't listen to anyone—"

"I didn't say that," the duchess interjected.

The prince grinned mischievously. "There is someone he can never say no to—my great-grandmother. The dowager queen is formidable when she chooses to intercede in a matter." He grimaced. "The problem is that she is in great mourning right now. She hasn't had visitors or come out of her suite in many weeks."

"That is true," the duchess added. "She's lost the lady who was her one true love. I can't imagine losing Soren, and for the queen, it was a love that spanned decades."

Prince Ronan sniffed. "I worry that she's given up on life herself."

"I don't know Dowager Queen Margrette as you do, but it seems to me she needs something to make her feel that she still matters. If she is Lord Windham's best chance for freedom, we must try."

"Yes!" The prince stood. "It's a good plan—and leave it to me to get an audience with her. She's always had a soft spot for me," he added cheekily. He scrutinized Rory. "Kexen, you'll need to do something about what Lady Windham is going to wear. He needs to look like the nobleman he is. Something along the lines of Taryn's clothes, I think."

"Hmm." Lady Tentrees eyed him with the same intensity. "I think you're right."

"Excellent." The duchess stood with excitement written across his face. "Let us make haste. The king could make his decision at any time, although I think he'll give himself until tomorrow to announce it."

Rory didn't know what to say, except, "Thank you. I've never had friends before. I hope it's not too forward for me to call you such," he added quickly.

The duchess pulled him into a hug. "Of course we are. Now, let's get you to my bed chamber so that Kexen can work his magic."

* * * *

Rory felt surprisingly comfortable in the long tunic and snug trousers that Kexen and Taryn had dressed him in, with Ronan adding his opinion when he'd returned from securing the audience with the dowager queen. They insisted on his using their given names, and as they'd plotted, he found his appetite had come back...as well as his determination. He was still not entirely convinced that the others were right about Evan loving him, but regardless, he was going to help set the man free, whether he liked it or not.

As the most senior of them, Ronan led the way. The guards on either side of the double doors at the end of the corridor straightened at his arrival and silently let them in. It was the most feminine place he'd been in since his mother's death, filled with ladies doing all manner of gentlewomen pursuits and all decked out entirely in white. *They're in mourning.* He knew the custom, not that the baron had bothered after his mother's death. Life had gone on in all its color and excesses in the castle as if she hadn't been laid in her tomb the very next day.

He fingered the sides of his tunic, forcing himself to continue walking toward the formidable and ancient woman lounging on the sofa at the far end. He seemed to be the only one who was nervous, however. Ronan practically skipped up to his great-grandmother and kissed her on each of her pale cheeks. Her face softened as she greeted him in return. And she murmured kind words of welcome to Taryn and Kexen.

Then it was Rory's turn. He reminded himself that she was not his enemy. The worst that would happen is that she'd dismiss his request and send him on his way. He'd be no worse off, and at least he'd know he tried his best to free Evan. After a moment's indecision, he bowed in front of her, the skirt of his tunic billowing out. That seemed to be the right call.

"Lady Evander Windham, welcome to my bower."

"Thank you, your majesty."

"So many male brides. I never thought I'd see the day, but I'm glad I did." She looked over her shoulder at an empty window seat covered with a spray of white flowers. "It's high time for a female groom, I should think. Ah well," she sighed. "Sit, sit. We'll have tea."

Servants brought forth enough food for a small army. Rory took a cup of tea and nibbled on a small fruit tart, not wanting to be rude. His stomach jittered with nerves, and he had to bite his tongue as small-talk was made about the state of crops, who in the palace was courting whom and even the weather.

"Rory, is it?"

He started at the sudden attention of the queen. He swallowed his mouthful. "Yes, ma'am."

"That odious Baron Finley is your father…except that he's not. You're better off with Sir Rolf. He's a fierce and loyal soldier for both my grandsons. Finley is a weasel, always has been. Rotting in a dark hole wouldn't be a harsh enough fate for him, but order has to be maintained, and the king can't have it said that his own sister-by-marriage, his niece and by extension, his brother, let him get away with such cruelty and stealing. Treating him like he's merely an idiot is the best outcome for all."

"All except for my husband," Rory dared to say.

Queen Margrette gave him first a stern look that turned his guts to water, then a sympathetic one. "Yes, he won't be the first sacrifice to a king's more important needs."

Rory's heart sank at that statement.

"Not that such an outcome is set in stone." She stared off into the distance as she sipped her tea. "I always thought him an impulsive boy—your husband. Charming as sin, too, of course. Even I wasn't immune to his cocky ways. Got himself into a pickle here, though, didn't he." She shook her head, then drained her cup and handed it off to one of her ladies who was hovering nearby.

Putting down his cup, Rory gathered his courage. "Your majesty, I don't want to cause any trouble in your family, but I love my husband, and the thought of living my life without him is a pain I don't think I can bear."

The woman looked at that empty seat again. "I know that feeling. It's different when you love them. Losing a husband and my sons as I did before their time was excruciating but Elspeth... There isn't a word that suffices." She took in a large breath and let it out slowly. "I will speak to the king. You have had so little time with your love. I would want you to have as much as you can. Besides," she added with a sly grin, "I think I know of a more fitting punishment for the rogue than laboring in the mines."

* * * *

"Do you think they're sending us to the mines?"

Evan gave Nemo the side-eye as the guards muscled them along. "Perhaps. Although if anyone thinks you can be held for long somewhere you don't want to be, they are fooling themselves. You are like smoke when you want to be." He leaned into them as much as the guard's hold would allow. "And you better not stay out of loyalty to me."

Nemo tossed their head in dismissal.

Why do I even try? There was no controlling Nemo, so he turned his attention to his wife. He wasn't sure if he hoped to catch sight of the boy or not. He'd done his best to push Rory away and should want him to be anywhere other than the throne room. Given his status, Evan had no doubt the king would deliver his verdict in person. Rory didn't need to hear that. There was nothing for the boy to do about it, and Evan could only hope that Soren, Rolf and the others already had a plan to help Rory forget he even had a husband. And while it was rare, they could possibly petition the king to dissolve the marriage. That would be the best outcome, a way for Rory to find another man to make him happy.

Of course I'd have to find a way to escape the mines and kill the fucker. No, that was not helping. He had no right to be possessive and selfish. He'd made this bad bed and would lie in it as an honorable man should.

As usual, the throne room was filled to the rafters with courtiers and gawkers who had nothing better to do than watch the theater of the king meting out punishment to a nobleman. This whole saga would be the topic of conversation for at least the next year. He did his best to keep his head high and his expression neutral. Anyone who'd come hoping to see him beg and weep or yell and curse would be sorely disappointed. As was he, damn it, when Rory was nowhere to be seen.

Good. That's the way I want it.

He bowed before the king, as did Nemo, although they did it so casually that everyone could tell that they didn't care about courtly manners.

The king didn't waste any time. "Release that ruffian. I have no doubt that Lord Windham has gained great loyalty, and I won't hold it against anyone."

Nemo turned to grimace at Evan. He silently pleaded with them to scram. And when that didn't work, he whispered, "Take care of Rory for me."

That did it, Nemo turned on their heel and stomped away in a very un-Nemo-like fashion. Evan turned his attention back to the king. "Thank you, sire."

"That's the last thing you'll thank me for. I have given your fate a great deal of thought and have received any number of…suggestions as to the best course of action to take with you." The man nearly squirmed with agitation. "Lady Windham, come forward."

Evan closed his eyes briefly, then opened them to see his wife arrive at his side. The boy was lovely, fetching as always but also regal-looking in a long-sleeved tunic made of green silk that skimmed his ankles. Snug trousers peeked through slits in the sides. Evan's fingers itched with the desire to snake their way through and run his hands down what he knew to be slender legs. Shockingly, he was becoming aroused in front of the entire court.

Pulling himself together, he stared at the king. "I do not want him here, your majesty."

"You've had far too much of what you wanted, Evander. Now it's my turn. Your wife is here because I ordered him to be. Now shut up and appreciate how lenient I'm about to be with you.

"Your offense was grave and unnecessary, given that there were other, legal solutions. However, I also recognize that your intentions were noble. You saved lives, and that can't be discounted. On the other hand, many who were only peripherally involved in the baron's...*mistakes* were robbed of what was theirs. Your toiling in the mines will not rectify their grievances. Therefore, I hereby sentence you to a lifetime of stewardship of the Windham lands. You will oversee them for your niece and will donate ten percent of the generous stipend she is willing to give you in order to make restitution to all your victims."

Evan was dumbfounded. In his wildest dreams, he'd never expected such an outcome, and he wasn't sure how he felt about it. Except of course, he did. He only had to look at his wife to know that spending the rest of his life tied to a castle was a far better choice than working to death in the mines, if for no other reason than Rory would be with him.

"Is this what you want?" It was bad form to ignore the king in favor of his wife, but he didn't give a damn. After the awful things he'd said to Rory in the dungeon, he didn't think the boy would welcome a life with him anymore.

Rory didn't even look at him as he answered. "Don't be stupid. Of course it is."

He blinked a few times at the biting tone before breaking out in a smile. He bowed to the king. "Sire, I humbly accept your judgment. You are showing me more mercy than I deserve. And," he added as a thought suddenly occurred to him, "I would ask for a favor, as well."

"A favor! My gods, man, you have gigantic balls. Sorry, my dear," the man said to the queen sitting next to him. She smiled serenely back at him and gave a simple nod. "Very well, what is it?"

"I should like your permission to marry my wife, again. He deserves something better than the hasty ceremony we had in the forest and a better wedding bed than the scruffy pallet I had to offer."

The little gasp Rory gave and the way he sneaked his hand over to clasp Evan's told him he'd done the right thing.

The king sighed. "Very well. Just keep it simple and private. I'm sure my grandmother will be pleased with the idea," he murmured.

The smug grin that flashed on Rory's face explained everything. Evan wanted to snatch him up and kiss him right then and there. Not wanting to strain the king's patience any longer, he bowed and tugged his wife away. "Come on, darling. We have a wedding to plan."

* * * *

Rory took one more look at himself in Taryn's long mirror. Unlike with his first ceremony, he was going to his wedding dressed in the finest white silk and lace he'd ever seen. How Kexen had coaxed such clothing out of the palace seamstress in such little time was a wonder. Yet, here he was, covered from neck to feet in a long tunic with bell sleeves, trousers gathered at his ankles and low white leather boots. His hair was pulled back in a complex braid entwined with a white, silk cord. He'd put his foot down about enhancing his face with some cosmetics, but Kexen took the loss with good grace. All three of his new friends stood around him with admiring expressions.

"I guess I'm ready." He put his palm to his stomach. "Why am I so nervous? It's not like I haven't been bedded by the man already." The others had insisted that he spend the last two nights apart from his husband, and Evan had agreed. It was a silly, romantic gesture, but it meant he was both anxious for the day to come and keen to get his hands on his husband again.

Taryn linked his arm with his. "Don't worry. From what Soren has told me, Evander has been pawing at the floor of your chamber like a stallion waiting to be put out to stud. You'll both be fine. How could you not with the love there is between you?"

Rory wasn't so sure that was true. He knew how he felt, but Evan was hard to read. His hurtful words could be dismissed as his stupid attempt to protect him from hurt. That didn't mean he had the same romantic feelings as Rory did. A marriage filled with affection and physical passion wouldn't be bad. It was simply that Rory wanted more. After a life of misery, he should be grateful for anything better than that. Somehow, he wasn't, and Evan had only himself to blame. He'd made Rory feel as if he mattered and had convinced him he deserved everything he'd dared dreamed about.

As commanded by the king, the wedding was small and mostly limited to the family—and that included Rolf. The man was waiting for him at the bottom of the staircase leading down to the private family garden. He looked handsome and important in his formal clothing. His smile when he caught sight of Rory gave his pride and confidence a boost. It was weird how he'd spent so many years wishing he had no father at all to looking forward to building a relationship with the man who had publicly claimed him.

Rolf took his arm. "Forgive me for saying that you are beautiful. Perhaps that is not what a son wants to hear."

Rory gave into an impulse to kiss the man on the cheek. "It's the perfect compliment. Thank you."

"Here." The man gave him a wide, gold band. "I assume you had nothing to give your husband the first time."

"Oh, thank you!"

"And I took the prerogative of a father and negotiated a marriage contract on your behalf. I'll go over it whenever you want. You'll be independent and in control of your life from now on."

"I appreciate it, but I trust you and Evan. I don't need to know what it says to be assured of that."

There was no more talking then. Rolf escorted him to the gazebo that had been decked out with flowers. It was beautiful, but he didn't think any more so than the one the brigands had created for him. He wished they could all be there. As it was, he was glad to see not only Evan's family, but also Maxwell and Nemo—and Kexen with his husband and even Prince Ronan and his mountain man. Everyone was in a festive mood. And there, standing beside Brother Manfred, was Evan. He, too, was dressed in a fine tunic and trousers and black boots polished to a high gleam. The highwayman was gone, and in his place was the nobleman Evander of Windham really was.

When Rolf handed Rory off to Evan, he took his hand and brought it to his lips. "You are even lovelier than you were the first time I married you."

"I don't expect that is a hard thing to do."

Evan scowled at him. "If you are to continue to be my wife, you must learn to respect yourself as I do. Are we clear on that?"

Rory grinned, his heart bursting with love. "Yes, my lord."

Brother Manfred cleared his throat. "Then let us begin."

* * * *

Rory lay unabashedly naked in the bed, just as his husband had put him. He was achingly hard for the man and eagerly watched as he stripped down to his own skin. It took him seconds, as always, and while he was now without clothes, he wasn't entirely nude. The ring Rory had slipped on his fingers winked in the sunlight streaming through the window. His heart tripped at the sight of the mark that proclaimed the man as his. And so, too, did he love gazing at the more delicate band Evan had surprised him with as they'd renewed their vows.

It was strange to be cloistered in their room, knowing that everyone else was down in the garden having a celebratory picnic. But such was the custom, and really, the thought of having to make small-talk with others before getting his hands on his husband again made him glad of it.

Rory let his hunger show as his husband approached, his big cock leading the way. "Come join me." He held out his hands and wrapped his arms around Evan as he took him into his embrace and covered his mouth.

The kiss was long and deep, the mating of their tongues a prelude to the mounting to come. Rory thought he could climax from this alone. In fact, his dick swelled and gave every sign of doing just that. It was he who reached between their bodies and clamped his fist around the base.

He broke off the kiss. "I want to try something, husband. Will you let me?"

Evan nipped his lower lip, then lapped it, before answering. "There is no 'let', darling. You may do what you wish on our bed."

Rory pushed him away and slithered out from under him. "Good, because I want you on your back." He knelt by him as he complied. "This time, I get to make love to you." Was it too soon to use such an expression? He resolved not to worry about it. The time had come to be more assertive and less afraid.

Evan lay with his arms by his side. "Is this how you want me?"

"Yes. No, spread your legs."

Once Evan did so, Rory positioned himself in the V Evan had made and took the man's cock with one hand. Evan groaned and bucked into the fist.

"Don't move. And you can't come until I give you permission."

Evan's eyes widened before closing to half-mast. "Whatever you say, my lady."

Rory gently played with the shaft, getting a feel for it and working up the courage for what he really wanted. Bracing himself on one palm beside Evan's hip, he leaned over and licked the tip of the cock. It jumped in his hold, and Evan grunted but otherwise made no move. Emboldened, Rory did it again, running his tongue along the slit. Salty pre-cum exploded on his tongue. He loved it, not because of the taste but because it proved he had the desired effect on his husband.

With increasing confidence, he licked the shaft from root to tip, then back again. He lapped around the balls as Evan did for him. The breathy groans and jerks of his husband's hips was most gratifying. Although he knew he could never fit the entirety of the dick in his mouth, he opened wide and took what he could. The hot and heavy cock sat on his tongue. He licked around it and sucked until he felt it start to swell. Clamping down on the base of the dick, he pulled away from it.

"I didn't give you permission to come yet."

Evan grunted with obvious frustration.

"It will be worth the wait. Trust me," he added, scraping his teeth ever so gently across the cockhead.

"Good gods!" Evan grimaced and fisted the bedding.

"Stay still." Rory slid off the bed and went to the table where their own wedding feast was spread out. Grabbing a cruet of oil, he raced back to the bed. He should have thought of this sooner, but he was sure Evan had behaved for these few seconds. And he had. His dick still stood up, glistening from a mix of Rory's saliva and the pre-cum that dribbled out.

Neither of those fluids would be enough, he knew. So he climbed back to his place between his husband's legs and tipping some oil onto the erection, he smothered the shaft with it. His own cock strained with eagerness. He badly wanted to come but not before he had his husband all the way in him. He let the cruet fall onto the bed, not caring that it spilled. His need to be filled was too great.

"I'm going to put you inside me now and ride you. Stay still and remember, you can only come when I say so."

Evan looked at him with fierce eyes. "You are killing me, wife."

Rory grinned. "Good." He wiggled his way into position, straddling Evan's hips now, his own legs spread as wide as they could go. Placing the man's cock against his hole, he pushed down. Aroused as he was, it burned from lack of prepping, but he didn't care. The pain was a reminder of the enormous pleasure to come. He bore down until Evan's cock was balls deep in his ass.

He shuddered at the feel of being filled to bursting. Closing his eyes, he commanded his husband. "Jerk me."

Evan didn't hesitate, gripping Rory's shaft and pulling it up and down with sure strokes. Rory began to rock, rising and falling with undulating hips, squeezing the dick inside him with as much force as he could. The pain faded and in its place was the glorious spark that spread out to every limb and made him come in his husband's hand. Seconds later, his channel was pushed wider as warmth bathed it. He hoped it would always be this—a simultaneous orgasm that joined them as nothing else could.

"I love you!" He shouted out his confession without thought and no regret. He'd laid himself bare to his husband in so many ways. How could he hold back this most important part.

In an instant he was on his back, Evan thrusting into him. "Say it again."

Rory opened his eyes to see his husband's heated stare. "I love you."

Evan fucked him with hard and fast strokes, as if he hadn't just come only moments before. Rory grabbed his shoulders and clung to him, as each thrust sent him sliding up toward the headboard. It was Evan's strong grip on his shoulders as he ravaged his mouth that kept him in place. They came again, together, their combined cries echoing down their throats.

As they panted and shook from the aftershocks of their orgasms, "Say it again," Evan demanded in a whisper.

"I love you." Rory pecked a kiss to the man's cheek. "I always will."

His husband pressed their foreheads together. "And I will always love you."

Rory's breath caught. "You don't have—"

"You're not going to argue with me, are you, wife?"

"No."

"Excellent, because I say what I mean, and you'll have to get used to hearing these words over and over again. I love you, Rory Windham."

He believed him, because for the first time in his life Rory had a name he could be proud of and a future to look forward to. Everything Evan had stolen from him he'd given back—and more. So much more that he would never feel alone or helpless again.

Epilogue

Evan ran his fingers over the effigy of his sister. "I am sorry, Merida. I should have remembered the kind woman you were. I will make it up to you by being a good steward to our ancestral lands. I will make you proud of me."

Rory slid his arm through Evan's. "Do you think she can hear you?"

"I don't know. I can hear myself, though, and I won't break my promise. Come… The others are waiting."

He led his wife to where their horse awaited them for the journey to Windham. With the coin his niece had given him, he could treat his wife to nights of comfort in inns instead of the hard ground. It felt good to be able to give the sweet boy everything he deserved.

He approached Manfred and held out his hand. "I'm pleased that you found a sympathetic ear in the abbot here. When you have done what you need to, I hope you'll consider making Windham your home. I, for one, could use your wise counsel."

Manfred shook his hand enthusiastically. "I can think of nothing better to do than keep you in line." He glanced at Rory. "Although I expect your wife can be counted on to do that."

Evan led Rory to Maxwell and Nemo next. "You are both welcome, as well. Maurice, too, of course, and all the others. Please tell them when you catch up to them. I owe them a good life without the danger they've faced with me these many years."

Maxwell bowed. "I would be honored to serve you and my young master...if that is what Maurice wishes. With you as his protector, I know I have discharged my promise to Lady Windham's mother. But I'm also selfish enough to want to carve out a life for myself." The man seemed abashed when Rory suddenly hugged him.

"I'm sorry I was so horrid to you. I should have understood that you had no more choice in what you did than I did."

"I always knew there was kindness in you. You just had to be given a chance to let that part of you out."

Nemo scowled at Evan when he turned his attention to them. "If you try to hug me, I'll break both of your arms. And I'd hate to burden your wife with that."

"I had no intention of doing so. You will come, too, yes?"

"Maybe. I'm not good as an indoor pet. You know that about me."

"Yes, and you know that I have never thought of you as an inferior. Come and go as you please. It will ease my mind to know you have a safe place to come to when you want."

"I'll see the others settled and maybe I'll stick around."

"Thank you." He really meant it. The fate of the others would weigh on his mind until he had them under his roof. Well, his niece's, really, but that was a quibbling matter. The king had provided a blanket pardon for all of them, so it was only a matter of making sure his band was happy, well-fed and secure.

They waited until the others left before mounting their own horses. He was rather disappointed that there was no reason for Rory to share one with him. He would miss the press of his pert ass against his groin. Ah well, there would be plenty of time to satisfy them both at each stop.

"Are you ready, darling?"

"Yes." Rory frowned.

Evan was a little alarmed. "What is it?"

"Nothing. Only…are you going to be bored to tears and miserable stewarding your niece's lands?"

"Of course I'm going to be bored," he said with a toss of his head. "It holds no more appeal than it did when my sister first asked me to. But miserable?" He shook his head and leaning over his horse, kissed his wife with all the love he could. "Never. Not with you by my side. Come on, darling. The road calls to us."

Want to see more from this author? Here's a taster for you to enjoy!

Treaty Brides: The Cordial Bride

Samantha Cayto

Coming October 2023

Excerpt

"When are we going to be there, Mama?"

Ian, Count of Charteris, smiled at his niece's plaintive question. He'd lost track of how many times she'd asked since their journey had begun a few days back. He flashed a smile at his sister. "Yes, when *are* we going to be there, *Mama*?"

Isabeau gave him her usual steely stare. Although she was the younger of them by a couple of years, she had adopted their mother's stern demeanor early in life. She turned her head toward her daughter, for whom she offered a gentler expression. "I believe we crossed the border into Shadow Valley moments ago. It shouldn't be long now until we reach our destination, but if I get that question one more time, Amalie, I shall send you to ride with your nurse."

Amalie rolled her eyes at Ian before saying, "Yes, Mama."

"Good." Isabeau returned her attention to Ian. "And I will take no more nonsense from you, brother. You're the one who volunteered to come on this diplomatic mission. If you're bored already, you have no one to blame but yourself."

"As if I would ever let my widowed sister and niece travel on their own to a foreign land with no treaty in place."

Isabeau pursed her lips. "We're not helpless, Ian, and the king has sent plenty of stout soldiers to protect us."

That was true. They were being accompanied by a few dozen of the king's finest, including two women who nearly dwarfed him in size, to be personal protectors of his sister and niece. He couldn't fault the security, yet there had been no question he would come once he'd heard news of his sister's appointment as special envoy. It was a proud accomplishment for Isabeau, he knew, but it didn't change the fact that the people living in Shadow Valley were unknown to them, and he'd be damned if he went about his merry way while the only two relatives he had left in the world headed into possible danger.

Not wanting to worry his niece in particular, he effected a causal attitude. "Think of this as you're doing me a favor, getting me out into the world and broadening my horizons."

Isabeau snorted, an unladylike sound that reminded him she was still the bold girl who'd followed him into all the mischief he'd made in their childhood and not just the staid matron that she'd become since marriage. "As if you've ever wanted to venture beyond the Charteris lands. I thought you'd break out into hives when you came to court to ask the king's permission to accompany me."

Ian didn't bother to correct his sister's impression of how his meeting with the king had gone. 'Asking' was not exactly how he'd characterize what he'd said to the man. There had never been any question as to his coming along. He looked out the nearest window of the carriage at the rolling valley beyond the thicket of trees lining the road. "This is hardly like being in the city. I quite like what I can see so far. Shadow Valley reminds me a bit of home, truth be told."

"It is lovely," his sister agreed. "But I know how much you like getting your hands dirty, and there will be none of that physical labor for you here. As my escort, you will be expected to act as a courtier. Be prepared for the tedium of long meals and mindless chatter."

Ian sighed. "I am." He would hate every minute of the diplomatic dance, but their father had instilled in him his duty to his female relatives. And because he loved these two females more than his own life, escorting them was no hardship.

Isabeau made a noise that indicated how little she believed his reassurance. Then her face lit up. "I suppose it's possible you might finally find your bride here. A marriage would do wonders for a treaty, as well."

Ian didn't bother to sugar-coat his thoughts on *that* topic. "Not going to happen, sister dear. I don't know how many more times I can tell you that I'm *not* going to marry—ever."

"Oh, such nonsense! Really, Ian, you hold a noble title and have a duty to produce an heir."

"I already have one." He winked at Amalie, who listened avidly at their conversation. If nothing else, it broke up the tedium.

Isabeau patted her daughter's hand. "Amalie already has the Truehart estate from her late father. Charteris and the title should go to a child of yours."

This was an old topic of conversation and one that he had little appetite to continue. He stretched his legs as best he could in search of a more comfortable position instead of arguing the point. Carriages were not made for large men. While his sister and niece shared one of the squabs with room to spare, the one he occupied across from them felt like a slightly soft instrument of torture. He would have made the journey on horseback but for his need to stick close to his cherished relatives. If danger made its way past the outriders, he would be the last defense. Gazing at the lushness of the country they entered, it was hard to believe that anything bad happened here. Everything was bright and colorful, with sun shining down to bathe it all in ethereal light. As a man who reveled in being outdoors, he thought he might find this trip enjoyable after all.

"Mama, I need a break, please." This was Amalie's delicate way of saying she needed to pee.

Truth be told, so did Ian. It would be a nice opportunity to stretch his legs, as well. The journey might be drawing to a close, but he knew their destination to the seat of Shadow Valley's ruling council was a way past the border. He rapped on the roof of the carriage to signal the drivers to stop. A few moments later, they did. Ian waited until the lead soldier shouted orders for his men to fan out to keep watch before opening the carriage door. He stepped out first, nearly groaning with relief, before handing his sister down. She stood to one side, shaking out her voluminous skirt as he lifted Amalie by her waist to set her beside her mother. The child was ten now, and it was disconcerting to notice how much she was heading into womanhood already. She bobbed a curtsy in thanks before her nurse came up from the carriage behind them to take her by the hand. His sister's maid was close behind to serve her mistress' needs.

Ian scanned the area for any sign of danger before saying, "I'll be nearby if you need me."

Isabeau waved him off before turning to join Amalie and the other women. Ian walked in the opposite direction to find a private spot to relieve himself. Beyond a stand of trees, he came upon a lovely lake with crystal clear blue water and a small outcrop of rocks across the way. He took a deep breath of the clean, sweet-smelling air as he undid his laces to release his dick, and turned his face into the heat of the sun. Shadow Valley was poorly named if this bit of it was representative of the whole country. A movement by the rocks caught his attention. He had his sword out of its scabbard in an instant. In the next one, he relaxed as someone came into view. No, not someone, a vision of beauty that overtook the landscape around them.

Ian had grown up on tales of woodland folk—fairies...beautiful creatures who flitted about the natural part of the world that they called home. For one wild moment, he thought they had been more than mere stories, that such otherworldly beings really did exist. It was a fanciful thought but not surprising, given the pale, slender boy with long, golden hair standing gloriously naked on top of the rocks. Even at a distance, his beauty was arresting, and he might have been mistaken for a girl if not for his obvious maleness on display. With amazing grace, the boy lifted his arms and dove into the water.

Ian followed the arc of movement with his gaze, then moved for a closer look when the boy didn't immediately come back up. Something bright flashed under the water before breaking through to the surface with splash. As Ian stood by the bank, staring like a fool, the pretty boy shook his head and dragged his wet hair away from his face with his fingers. He treaded water and grinned at Ian. His gaze flicked downward, and his grin grew wider.

It took Ian a moment to realize he'd forgotten to re-sheath his sword and do up his laces. It its unconfined state, his dick had no trouble standing, hard and eager, signaling the instant desire he had felt at the first sight of this water nymph. He carefully put away his sword so that he didn't accidently castrate himself. But when he grabbed his cock to stuff it back into his trousers, the boy gave a cheeky wave before diving back under. The sight of a slick, small rump hovering above the surface before submerging had Ian coming with a surprised grunt. He'd been careful not to tend to this need during the journey out of respect for his sister. His dick had been unable to behave itself in the face of such bold temptation, however. His seed spilled on the ground, leaving him nearly dizzy with the force of it.

He stood staring long after the tremors of his climax had subsided and his dick softened enough to be confined back behind his laces where it belonged. Like some sappy young man, he longed for another glimpse of the boy. It wasn't until he his sister's voice calling to him cut through the fog of desire that he pulled himself together and headed back to the road. Still, he couldn't resist a glance over his shoulder. There was nothing to see except the nature around him. It was almost as if he'd imagined the whole encounter.

Except he hadn't.

* * * *

Calan raced home, letting the wind dry his hair as his horse galloped across the fields. It had been naughty of him to indulge in his whim for a ride and a swim in the lake. His aunt had stressed repeatedly that he had to be ready to greet the strangers who were expected any time now. As a member of the ruling council, she had to be part of the welcoming party, and as her only relative, he was required to hover in the background in support of her. All the rules of etiquette bored him silly. He much preferred being out and about, exploring their land and working in the garden. That was where his true talent lay. Stuffing him into his best clothes and forcing him to socialize was torturous for him and of no value to his people. A possible treaty with the mighty Moorcondia was important to Shadow Valley, to be sure, but no one should be counting on *him* to help with that endeavor. He had no diplomatic skills and was terrible at making small talk.

As he arrived at the stables, his mind wandered back to what had happened by the lake, however. He had very likely been the first of his people to make an impression on one of their guests. And although he was inexperienced in the ways of sex, he knew enough to understand he'd made a very *good* impression on the man, at least. Just the thought of the large, hard cock waving at him sent his own dick and balls tingling. He forced a stop to his burgeoning arousal. There was no time for that nonsense. He contented himself with the knowledge that he would soon see the man again up close. There was no way he was merely a soldier, not given his mode of dress. Because Calan knew the Moorcondian envoy was a woman, he wondered who the man was. *Her husband, no doubt.* A pity. It would have been nice to at least flirt with such a handsome and powerful-looking man. It would have been nicer still if Calan had finally found a man who could deflower him without the sticky complications of seeing each other every day under his aunt's watchful eye.

There was no more time to dwell on it. His aunt called out his name in the tone of voice that warned him he was on the wrong side of her temper already. Calan handed his horse off to a stable boy, who gave him a sympathetic look before heading for the barn. Knowing that any further delay would be to his detriment, Calan ran to the back door of the cottage he shared with his only living relative. Aunt Celia had raised him since his parents' death, and he really owed her respect and gratitude. He just wished she'd loosen up a little. Sometimes he worried that she'd crumble to tiny bits if her hard façade was cracked even a small amount. She was implacable on everything and was not happy at the prospect of forming a treaty with any country. Everyone knew that she'd opposed the vote to accept Moorcondia's overture, vociferously so. But she also did her duty, no matter her personal feelings. His tardiness couldn't be helping what had to be already-fraught nerves.

He raced to where she stood, tapping her toes. "Sorry, Aunt. I lost track of time. I won't be more than another moment." He slipped past her to enter the cottage, feeling the lash of her tongue, despite her silence.

It didn't take long for him to make himself presentable. His swim in the lake had left him clean and refreshed, and he didn't have many clothes. He donned his good tunic and trousers in the light blue color that he was vain enough to think set off the color of his eyes to good effect and belted it with the leather braid he'd made himself. His good brown boots were already polished to as glossy a shine as he could manage, so all that was left to do was fix his hair. He braided it into a tail that hung over his shoulder as he hurried back down to his waiting aunt. With a quick grin, he stood for inspection.

Aunt Celia gave a curt nod. "You'll do." Her own attire was its usual simple black gown with only a green beaded belt to give it any color. She wore her hair in such a severe bun that her face always looked as if it might split in two if she twitched a smile—which she rarely did and never for long. "Come along. The sentries have already sounded the alarm. Our *guests* are about to arrive."

Calan followed a half-step behind her, always the dutiful nephew in public. It didn't take long to arrive at the longhouse. Celia's high station meant she had a house near to the square that served as the hub of their people. A large crowd had already gathered, not surprising given the historic nature of the envoy's arrival. Shadow Valley wasn't exactly cut off from the rest of the world, but other than traders, they rarely saw people from neighboring lands. The prospect of doing a formal treaty with a country as powerful as Moorcondia was exciting—and frightening. His aunt and others who thought like she did warned that they would be overtaken if they didn't watch their step. Moorcondia might say they are looking for a treaty, but they could be scouting out a possible means of attack. Calan couldn't see the logic in that thinking. If the man he'd seen was any indication, the Moorcondians looked to be powerful enough to conquer them without subterfuge.

They joined the rest of the council and their families by the entrance to the longhouse. Everyone was dressed in their finest clothes and every pair of eyes was trained on the direction their guests were arriving from. The sound of horse hooves heralded the

Moorcondians' arrival. Then a line of large soldiers came into view. There was a collective gasp and some murmurs at the sight. It was impressive and scary. Although none of the men had weapons drawn or were doing anything menacing, it was obvious how that could change in a moment. But then a beautiful carriage followed, and now the reaction of his people was more like awe. That conveyance was large and covered in colorful heraldic signs and gilded edges. If nothing else, these strangers were displaying their wealth. More men and another, less elaborate carriage, followed. The entire procession pulled up in front of the longhouse. Now the crowd had gone silent as everyone watched and waited for what was to come next.

A soldier dismounted and opened the door of the first carriage. Calan was probably the only one what wasn't surprised to see a large man emerge from the conveyance first. Up close, he was even more impressive than he'd been by the lake. He was easily a head taller than the average Shadow Valley man, which Calan couldn't count himself among. He would barely reach the top of this man's chest, not that such a measurement would ever be made, he quickly reminded himself. The Moorcondian was the epitome of masculine beauty, with a square jaw, long, straight nose and high cheek bones. His light-brown hair was styled in a casual mess of waves that skimmed his shoulders. Like Aunt Celia, he was dressed entirely in black, but these clothes had style, with golden embroidery along the collar, cuffs and hem, and his knee-high black boots shined more brightly than Calan could ever achieve with his own. And there was a sword belted at his waist—something Calan had barely noticed by the lake, distracted as he'd been by the man's cock—but the weapon was also obviously not merely for decoration. This was a soldier as well as an aristocrat, that much was obvious.

The Moorcondian man stood for a second, scanning the crowd, His gaze skimmed over Calan, then returned quickly to bore a hole into him. Calan's cheeks heated under the scrutiny of dark eyes, and when the man smiled oh so briefly, a strange warmth settled in Calan's groin. It was a relief when the man turned his attention back to the carriage. He offered his hand to someone inside and a woman alighted a moment later. This was the envoy, and she was every bit as interesting, although Calan wasn't attracted to women. Unlike everyone else so far, she was dressed in bright colors of yellow and gold. Her gown had a full skirt the likes of which Calan had never seen before. Obviously, she did no physical labor. She had the same look about her as the man, except her hair was mostly covered by an elaborate type of kerchief that had a bejeweled band above her brow.

The woman smiled brightly as she headed toward the leader of the council. There was nothing in particular that caused Fennic to stand out as such, yet this diplomat obviously had a trained eye. She curtsied in front of him. "My lord, Fennic, thank you for greeting me."

Momentarily flustered, Fennic flicked his gaze around before giving a shallow bow. "Lady Isabeau, it is my great pleasure. And please, call me Councilor. We have no lords or ladies here, only elected members of our governing body. It is my humble duty to hold the headship for a few more years yet."

Lady Isabeau's smile didn't waver. "Of course, Councilor. Your manner of government is one of the many intriguing aspects of your country that I hope to get to know better."

Pretty words, but everyone knew that Moorcondia wasn't there for lessons in politics. It was rumors of their most recent cordial that had precipitated this overture. Shadow Valley had the best medicines, given its diverse flora. Everyone knew that. But this latest concoction had the power to change people's lives by avoiding terrible death. Calan was all for sharing in the marvel, but it wasn't his decision to make, and the idea of the upcoming dance of negotiation he was sure would take place intimidated him. He had no skill at such things, nor was he interested in the ensuing introduction of the rest of the council, so he trained his focus on the man he assumed was the envoy's husband.

Fortunately, the Moorcondian wasn't looking at him. He'd turned his attention back to the carriage and lifted out of it a girl who was obviously the envoy's daughter. She was the spitting image of the woman, except her violet colored gown was simpler and her hair was uncovered. It was tamed in complex braids wound with silver ribbon. She was like a bright and beautiful creature among the more plainly dressed girls clinging to their mother's skirts as they watched the proceedings. Taking her by the hand, her father led her over to her mother.

Lady Isabeau gestured toward them. "May I introduce my daughter, Mistress Amalie Charteris Truehart of Truehart Manner." When the girl curtsied with the same grace as her mother had, the woman continued. "And this is my brother, Ian, Count of Charteris. He was keen to see your lovely country for himself, and our king kindly gave him permission to accompany me."

A weird sort of relief rushed through Calan. *Brother, not husband.* Now when the man glanced in his direction, Calan permitted himself to smile back at him.

He had little experience with flirting but hoped the man would understand that was what he was doing. The heated gaze he got in return told him he did.

The man sketched a bow to the council. "I hope my presence is acceptable to you. Since my sister is widowed, I thought it appropriate to escort her. Although as she implied," he added with another flick of his eyes in Calan's direction, "I am keen to explore the beauty of your land."

Fennic waved with open arms. "Of course, Count. You are most welcome, and no man here can fault your admirable concern for your sister's welfare. I assure you, however, that she and her lovely daughter are quite safe with us."

"Of course," the count agreed with an affable tone that nevertheless conveyed that his guard was not down.

Celia stepped forward. "If you care to enter our longhouse, Lady Isabeau, we have refreshments for you and your…entourage to partake in before we begin our discussions."

"How very kind. Thank you. And I look forward to discussing the many ways a treaty with Moorcondia can benefit both your people and ours."

Being a diplomat, she was careful not to mention the cordial, but everyone knew the rumors had spread about it and that was what had brought the woman here after many generations of their people knowing about each other.

Fennic nodded. "Indeed, we are also looking forward to it. This way, if you please." He led them through the doors.

The family members of the twelve councilors filed in behind them, leaving the rest of their people to go about their business. Normally, Calan hated these command performances of social interaction. This time, he was eager to be a part of things. It gave him a chance to get a better look at the count, although he was seated at the far end of the long communal table, and it was hard to do any more than glance at the man across the expanse of food between their two sides. And it might have been his imagination, but he could swear that the man was perusing him, as well. Every time Calan dared to look at him, he was staring back. Toward the end of the meal, the count even winked at him. Calan was wide-eyed with shock at the brazen flirtation and must have turned beet red, given how hot he felt. He realized he was out of his depth with a man like the count, so he kept his head down until everyone rose from the table.

Lady Isabeau said, "A delicious meal, Councilor Fennic. Thank you."

"You are most welcome. Shall we retire to the council room to begin our discussions?" Fennic gestured toward the door at the far end of the longhouse.

Only council members and those serving them refreshments ever entered it, but Calan knew, as everyone did, that it held a great round table to demonstrate that all the council members had equal power.

As curious as he was about the Moorcondian, Calan wanted the freedom that came from leaving. He needed time to get used to these new feelings of mutual attraction and was always happiest when wandering alone in nature. Before they were all dismissed, however, Lady Isabeau made a request.

"I wonder if it's possible for someone to show my daughter and brother some of your charming town? The journey was long, and a good walk would be appreciated."

"Of course." Fennic looked around for someone suitable.

Before he could ask anyone to perform that duty, the count interjected. "How about this young man?" He pointed at Calan. All heads turned in his direction, and he froze with the scrutiny.

Aunt Celia frowned. "That is my nephew, Calan. He is not part of the government and merely helps me with my work as a healer."

"Indeed?" The count smiled ingratiatingly. "Then he sounds like the perfect person to introduce me to your flora. I work my lands myself and have a keen interest in farming. With your permission of course, madam."

Aunt Celia was clearly not pleased with the idea, probably worried that Calan would give away the secret of their new cordial before the treaty was negotiated. She saw him as obtuse at the best of times, more interested in plants than people, and he didn't mind cultivating—sort to speak—that perception. He would never do such a thing, of course, unless he knew it was what the council wanted. The protection of Shadow Valley was every bit as important to him as it was to everyone else. Spending time close up and mostly privately with the man so soon after meeting him was a daunting idea, too, the complete opposite of what he'd just resolved to do. If he didn't take advantage of the forced opportunity, however, his virginal state might last forever.

He dared to step forward. "I would be delighted to, Aunt." He gave them all his best vacant expression, as if he had no more thoughts in his head than a butterfly.

Fennic intervened before Aunt Celia could respond. "An excellent suggestion."

The count held out his hand to his niece. "Marvelous. Come, Amalie."

The girl didn't hesitate to clasp hands with her uncle. Her nurse kept one step behind her. "What shall we see first?" she asked Calan. She was a far more self-assured child than he'd ever been.

The answer was easy, though. "The decorative gardens. They don't serve a usual purpose other than enjoyment, but I'm sure you'll like what there is to see." Calan let his gaze encompass the count.

The man's heated look back was unnerving. "I already do."

About the Author

Samantha Cayto is a Boston-area native who practices as a business lawyer by day while writing erotic romance at night—the steamier the better. She likes to push the envelope when it comes to writing about passion and is delighted other women agree that guy-on-guy sex is the hottest ever.

She lives a typical suburban life with her husband, three kids and four dogs. Her children don't understand why they can't read what she writes, but her husband is always willing to lend her a hand—and anything else—when she needs to choreograph a scene.

Samantha loves to hear from readers. You can find her contact information, website details and author profile page at https://www.pride-publishing.com

www.ingramcontent.com/pod-product-compliance
Lightning Source LLC
LaVergne TN
LVHW090941080826
845145LV00003B/837